Mind the Threefold Law you should, three times bad and three times good.

When misfortune is enow, wear the blue star on thy brow.

True in love ever be, lest thy lover's false to thee.

Eight words the Wiccan Rede fulfill: An ye harm none, do what ye will.

The Shadow Reigns

Witch-Hunter 2

K. S. Marsden

K.S.M

Printed by Amazon.com

Cover art: Sylermedia

ISBN-13: 978-1499298215
ISBN-10: 1499298218

An insight from our villain

For hundreds of years witches have been persecuted; forced to keep their heads down and conform to laws that we never agreed to. To be a witch is to live a hunted life; to suffer the stupidity and ignorance of those around you, even though you could outclass them with the simplest spell.

I was born to free the witches from oppression. I am the Shadow Witch. I have freed my kin from the so-called justice of the witch-hunters and their Malleus Maleficarum Council. In one night, the world was thrown into chaos, and for once it was the witch-hunters that were forced back.

We followed our victory with a second. We pitched the world into darkness and removed the advantage technology gave our enemies. The new world has already begun, and in this spiralling darkness, those with magic will finally be able to rise above all others.

Then why do I feel guilty? Why do I feel doubt?

Ever since the witches told me of my destiny, when I was thirteen and powerless, I have never felt any doubt in my path. When my powers were awakened seven years later – the witches conducting sacrifices on Hallowe'en to break the ancient spell holding them back – I was even more sure of what lay ahead.

But it is shallow of me to even pretend I do not know the reason that I finally question everything. Him. For years I hated the very name Astley, knowing that they were the witch-hunters that killed Sara Murray, the last Shadow Witch; and all its consequences. I would not be the same if she lived; I would not have to take up this brutal destiny.

I had not planned to fall in love with the current bearer of the name: George "Hunter" Astley. I ignored the attraction at first; whenever he was around, I told myself it was the excitement of playing him for a fool that thrilled me so, not his presence itself. But after months of secretly savouring each glance, each touch, I wanted more. I knew from the beginning that our relationship was doomed; I could not stay with him and soon we would be on the opposite sides of a war. Is it wrong I tried to find a way to keep him with me? If not for my sake, then for our child's?

Not that it mattered. In the end he chose his side, and I chose mine.

I knew that I was expected to kill him when we met again, and I was prepared to do so. I came so close and failed. As my knife got past his guard and cut deep into him, I felt a shock of pain stab through me. It was all I could do to evade his witch-hunters and return home, where I collapsed at my mother's feet.

I have been recovering slowly for a month now. I cannot explain it, there is no physical wound; I can only guess that what was inflicted on him rebounded to me. None of the witches can explain why, but some theorise that the child links us – we can only guess what powers he or she shall inherit. In which case, if this is true; I shall withdraw as much as possible until it is born and hope the spell breaks.

Chapter One

Little Hanting was a picturesque village in the English countryside. Quaint bungalows and farmhouses fanned out from the church hall, with its perfectly manicured green in front of it. Not that the grass could be seen; fresh snow had again fallen the previous night, coating everything with a perfect whiteness. All it needed was children with mittens having a snowball fight, and the scene would be idyllic.

But Little Hanting silently suffered. The inhabitants had all been evacuated when the village had been the setting for a decisive battle. Now all the homes lay eerily quiet, save for the ones that had been temporarily taken over by soldiers. They sheltered from the cold and waited – waited for answers and for their next move. They would huddle around the fireplaces, casting glances in the direction of the local manor house.

Hunter drifted in a haze of painkillers and nightmares. He saw the flash of the knife a hundred times, Sophie's hazel eyes, and the pain that tore through them both.

The scene would change, and it was Hunter's first day at University, and Brian was coming to tell him that his father was dead. Charlotte should be here to comfort him. Where was Charlotte?

When Hunter was awake... lucid was hardly applicable. He lay in his bed, staring at the high ceiling, with all its familiar cracks. Or he would turn his head to observe the dark drapes that someone opened and closed with the passing of day and night. Huh, probably the same someone that fed the fire in his bedroom to stop it being too cold.

Not that Hunter cared, the cold was numbing, and combined with the morphine, opium – whatever drug they managed to dredge up, it was a good haze. It stopped him having to think as much. Or at least, it kept his thoughts strangely disconnected from himself.

So, this was what it was like to wallow. Hunter had never been much of a wallower: not when the witches had killed his father; Brian; Charlotte... Hunter was a witch-hunter, as they all had been. It was accepted as fact that you would lose friends and family, that you yourself would be a target. To be a part of the Malleus Maleficarum Council, to protect the people from the violence of witches was to invite that violence onto oneself.

But the pain of the past was nothing compared to what he was putting off feeling now. It wasn't as if Sophie had died – although Hunter wished she had. No, it had been worse. The woman he loved had turned out to be the Shadow Witch. It sickened him to think of the nights spent together, the caresses, the half-asleep conversations. And the days when he had never doubted his trust in her as a colleague and a friend. How could she have acted so innocently and seemed so honest when she had just killed his old mentor and closest friend?

Before, grief had only driven him harder to fight back against witches. Now Hunter felt confusion over his life's work in eradicating witches. He had fallen in love with one, and now she carried his child; and Hunter had recently discovered his own magic-like abilities.

Hunter had thought Sophie mad, and looking for a loophole when she had sworn that he was different from his fellow witch-hunters.

It was something that Hunter, and every MMC worldwide took for granted that, in a family of witch-hunters, each generation would become more adept. By the 3rd gen they could perceive spells being cast, and were immune to some magic; as well as being stronger and faster. As an unheard of 7th gen, Hunter Astley had been revered by the MMC. How little everyone (including himself) knew that he would evolve into a magic-wielder.

Which left him with the question: should he use his new talents in this war; or should he copy the fabled Benandanti and kill himself for being a witch?

He had no answers, and the thoughts just swirled incessantly in his head while he tried to numb them.

The only thing that broke the cycle of monotonous thought was mealtimes. Usually someone left a coffee on his bedside table in a morning, although chances were that it would still be sitting there, stone-cold, by midday. And then someone would bring him some lunch.

This irritating someone came in the form of Hunter's best friend, James Bennett. He was a pretty average guy – average height, average brown hair and eyes. He was a little more intelligent than most. But this 1st gen witch-hunter was the truest and bravest person that Hunter knew. Oh, and James also had an invaluable knack for putting up with Hunter on a daily basis. Hunter couldn't remember a time when James hadn't been there for him.

Which included bringing him meals while Hunter was injured, it seemed. Hunter was never very hungry and would have left the unappetising food if James hadn't stayed. Not that James was watching and making sure his friend actually ate something. No, it just so happened that mealtimes coincided with James having found something interesting in the Astley library, and brought up one old book or another to get Hunter's opinion.

Twice a day. Every day.

Today was a little different. James sat with the typical book on his lap, and the non-typical red pointy hat on his head.

Hunter shot him a few looks, but today James was staying quiet. Hunter dutifully finished his soup and the last of the bread, pointedly putting the bowl aside to state it was empty.

"Why?" Hunter asked simply.

"Why what?" James returned innocently, looking up from his book.

Hunter sighed. "The hat?"

"Oh, that. I thought it'd annoy your mum." James replied with a shrug. "And it's my birthday. One of the soldiers found this and thought it wa' funny."

That made Hunter sit up and pay attention. "What? It's the end of January already? Oh shit, I'm sorry James, I forgot. It's just... it's been a blur, I lost track."

James shrugged again, but Hunter noticed the mischievous glint in his eye. "Hey, it's fine. We've all been preoccupied with somethin' a bit bigger than my birthday.

11

Besides, I distinctly remember you saying that if you forgot my birthday, I could have that bottle of '82 Chateau Gruard Larose that's in your cellar."

"Oh, I said that, did I?" Hunter tried to keep a straight face.

"Yep, absolutely." James replied sincerely, pushing the reading glasses back up his nose.

"Ok, so I get the hat. What's with the glasses?"

James looked a little surprised at the question. "Dunno, I just find it easier reading with them. Maybe the witches did some damage when they beat the crap out of me. Or maybe I should just admit I'm getting old."

Hunter snorted. "Twenty-five is not old. Oh, sorry, twenty-six now. Happy Birthday."

"I thought they made me look more intelligent." James continued.

"Well you couldn't look any less so." Hunter returned quickly.

James looked ready to throw his book at him, but seemed to think better of it. Instead, he got to his feet.

"Well, you seem back on form, Hunter. So perhaps you'll think about getting your arse out of bed. We've a war to plan. And we could do with your help in keeping Mrs Astley in check."

Hunter groaned, more at the mention of his mother than impending war.

"And you might want to shave." James added, eyeing the scruffy attempt of a beard his face was sporting. "Or not. I could be the handsome one, as well as the smart one."

With a chuckle, James turned and finally left.

Chapter Two

Hunter finally made it downstairs that afternoon, cleaned up, dressed, and looking much more his old self. The beard was gone, and his black hair combed into something resembling control. He'd managed to find a clean jumper and jeans, and looked presentable.

He was greeted by a warm chorus from a crowd of people in what used to be the dining room. Astley Manor had been in his family for nearly two hundred years; the image of extravagant Georgian architecture, it was comfort and luxury for the line of Astley witch-hunters. And the house had its own secrets, no witch could enter the Manor without their powers being stripped; no magic could be used in the extensive estate. The only exception being Hunter's anti-magic talents.

Which made it the perfect emergency home for the Malleus Maleficarum Council after the witches had destroyed their base. After their initial defeat, witch-hunters had trickled into Astley Manor, seeking safety, and planning their next attack.

Hunter was more than happy to open his home to his allies, but even the vast Astley Manor was not big enough to house them all, especially after the additional influx of soldiers for the last battle. Those that could not be made comfortable in the Manor stayed in the village and travelled in every day to learn of any progress made.

The over-crowding of the Manor was not universally welcomed. One in particular loathed it - Mrs Astley. Hunter's mother had always had very strict rules over protocol and etiquette, and this flooding of the Manor with all sorts insulted her deeply. The last straw was the dining room. After the witch-hunter hooligans converted that into a war room, Mrs Astley resigned to her rooms and refused to come out unless absolutely necessary.

At this very moment, about a dozen people sat around the large table, most of them nursing a fresh mug of tea. The two most senior stood up at Hunter's appearance.

"Mr Astley, it's good to see you up and about." General Hayworth smiled as he looked over Hunter, a touch of concern in his blue eyes.

"Thank you, General." Hunter replied, trying to hide how breathless he was from just coming downstairs. "My nurse has cleared me for duty again."

"Huh. Well, sit down before you fall down, Astley." 5th gen Anthony Marks said with a shake of his head.

Hunter smiled bitterly, embarrassed at how weak his body had become. He obediently took an empty seat and looked expectantly towards the two older men. "So, can you bring me up-to-date?"

General Hayworth returned to his chair and started first. "It's been three weeks since the battle, the witches must know about it by now and are giving us a wide berth. Communications are still down, so it's hard to get any real idea of what they're doing at this time. They are probably doing the same as us – assessing the situation and strengthening their forces."

"And how are our forces?"

Anthony Marks sighed. "Again, with no way of getting in touch quickly, we can only guess. Aside from the forty-seven witch-hunters that were in the battle, we've had others making their way here over the weeks. There's nearly a hundred now. We've housed them in Little Hanting alongside the soldiers. We have been sending out patrols to try and find more, but it's a slow process."

"This lack of technology is a pain in the arse." Hayworth interjected.

"That would be why they did it." Hunter muttered. He remembered Sophie gloating over the blanket of magic that disrupted most technology. Hunter and his colleagues had been thrown back into the dark ages, while Sophie and her witches had their magic to get by and make faster progress.

Marks frowned at Hunter's comment, but brushed over it. "We've started sourcing generators, most of them are in working condition, we've just got to keep an eye on fuel usage. Luckily the Manor was built before our dependency on technology, so no problems here. As for the MMC... the Council is destroyed. As the most senior member, I have officially assumed control. Until someone more senior steps up, of course."

Hunter grew uncomfortable under Marks' steady gaze. It was crazy – Anthony Marks was twice Hunter's age; Hunter had grown up hearing nothing but positive accounts of this witch-hunter from both his father and his trainer, Brian Lloyd. But because Hunter had been born an unheard of 7th gen, that automatically gave him superiority. All he had to do was claim it.

15

"I'm not going to do that, Mr Marks. I never wanted to lead."

General Hayworth chuckled at his comment. "Who the hell does want to take responsibility and lead? Especially now the world's screwed up." He looked over at Marks. "Looks like you're stuck with the gig, Anthony. Now, pay up."

Sighing, Anthony shifted in his seat and pulled a crumpled note out of his pocket, handing it reluctantly to Hayworth. Around the table there were a few more subtle exchanges.

"We had a little wager going on. Had to amuse ourselves somehow, waiting for you to pop up again." Hayworth grinned as he explained to Hunter.

Hunter wasn't sure how he felt about this amusement at his expense, but he let it slide. "I wouldn't trust myself to make the right decisions. I'm too close to this."

The room fell silent, and Hunter wondered how much these men knew. James knew everything, having gone right through it all with Hunter. The General knew an edited version that Hunter had shared with him before the battle, but how much more had he learnt? And how much did the others know, or guess?

"Fine." Marks finally said. "Well as your Head of Council, I need to know how soon you can start that travelling in a blink again. It would be a monumental advantage to have you cover so much ground. It'd also mean we can save our fuel rations for something more important."

Hunter stared down at the table, his 'blinking' still felt like a dirty secret. But at least these guys weren't preparing to burn him at the stake. Yet. "I need to build my strength again. I will keep you informed on my progress, sir."

16

"Good. You go do that. And, ah…" Marks pulled a face, which told Hunter exactly what he was going to bring up next. "Perhaps you should go see if you can placate your mother. She doesn't seem too chuffed to have us here."

Hunter nodded and, finding no reasonable excuse for putting it off until later, he promptly made his way to his mother's rooms.

Mrs Astley had a whole wing to herself, with a bedroom, office, drawing room and a large bathroom all for her private use. She liked having the space to herself, especially when her son insisted on bringing all sorts of waifs and strays to stay. Her space was even more important to her now that her home had been invaded and militarised.

Hunter rarely came to this part of the house. His mother was not his favourite person, he'd had very few reasons over the years to seek out her company. Especially as Mrs Astley would often pop up and interfere, whether she was welcome, or not.

Hunter turned the handle to her main room, pushing the door open and giving it a couple of sharp knocks to announce his presence. He walked into the expensively furnished drawing room, looking for his mad ol- dear, loving mother.

"Mother?" He called out.

"George, how many times must I tell you that it is common decency to wait for permission to enter." The familiar sharp tones snapped.

Hunter turned to see his mother, and their butler Charles, sitting by the window, playing chess.

"One of these days you will walk in while I am indisposed, and I daresay the embarrassment will be punishment enough." Mrs Astley added, her fingers hovering over a black rook, then finally making her move.

"I'm sorry, mother. I won't do it again." Hunter replied, wincing slightly at the image she provided.

"Of course, you'll do it again, you never learn from your mistakes – just like your father."

Ah yes, there it was. Hunter wondered if they could make it through a single conversation without his mother bringing up George "Young" Astley. Hunter worshipped the memory of his late father. His mother still blamed Young for ruining her life. She often wished he had left her to be sacrificed by witches, rather than give her this life. How many times had Hunter heard that over the years?

"I haven't seen you for a month, why have you been avoiding me this time?" Mrs Astley cut through her son's train of thought.

Hunter stared at her, wondering if she was really so ignorant to everything going on around her. "Mother, I've been an invalid. Laid up in bed for three weeks, recovering after Sophie tried to kill me."

"Oh." Mrs Astley finally looked away from her chess game to see her son. Her eyes ran quickly from head to toe, but seeing no real problem, she finally met his gaze. "Sophie, that common girl you were dating? Well, I did tell you not to bother with her."

Hunter clenched his fists and tried not to show how much his mother was winding him up right now. She told him not to bother with Sophie? Oh, so somehow Mrs Astley could tell that Sophie was evil, and the biggest threat this century? No, more likely the stuck-up Mrs Astley was offended by her son's interest in a "common" girl.

Mrs Astley sighed, reading her son's reaction. One that did not need an audience. "Charles, more tea."

The ever-dutiful Charles nodded, and stood up from the chess game, more than happy to leave the Astleys to yet another family interlude.

Once the butler had gone, Hunter drifted over to the table and chessboard that were set by the window, to get the most of the winter sun. He could see that Charles' white pieces could checkmate his mother in three moves. It wouldn't happen of course, Charles always let Mrs Astley win.

"Don't look at the board pretending you know how to play chess, George." Mrs Astley snapped.

"I do know how to play chess, mother. James taught me years ago." Hunter replied calmly.

"Oh, don't mention that odious boy!" Mrs Astley fumed, something about the Yorkshireman always seemed to rile her up. "He is still staying here, I presume? You should start charging him rent."

"Mother… things have changed. Witch-hunters need somewhere safe to stay." Hunter said, trying to change her way of looking at it.

"And that Marks fellow – running around like he owns this place! I imagine he always had his beady eye on the Manor, when he used to come visit Young. Now he goes and fills it with all sorts!"

Hunter waited impatiently for his mother's rant to end. "No mother, I own this place. And as lord of Astley Manor, I turned it into a centre of control for the MMC, I have encouraged witch-hunters to use it as a sanctuary. And I pushed Anthony Marks to take command."

Mrs Astley sat thin-lipped, considering this. "I am not sharing my rooms." She eventually announced.

"No one is asking you to, mother." Hunter replied with a touch of exasperation. "They are being housed in the village too, there's space enough."

"What?" Mrs Astley looked up at her son with surprise. "The villagers will not take kindly to you pushing house guests on them."

Hunter narrowed his eyes at his mother. "The villagers were evacuated three weeks ago to save them from the witches."

"Oh." Mrs Astley took this bit of news in. "So that must be why Mrs Harsmith has not been to visit. I assumed she had the flu again."

Hunter was caught at that familiar place between wanting to laugh at her and being thoroughly annoyed by her. He decided to take the safest path.

"I will leave you to your tea and chess, mother."

Chapter Three

"Oi Hunter, wake up!"

Hunter groaned and rolled over, tucking the warm sheets tighter about himself.

"Any time today mate."

Hunter cracked open one eye to see James hovering by his bedside, holding a candlestick for light. Funny how his family's stash of old-fashioned items were finding use again.

"What's this about, James?" Hunter croaked.

"We're going running this mornin'. Get up."

"What? What time is it?" Hunter asked, pushing himself to sit up in his bed.

"Nearly six am."

Hunter groaned. "Come back at a more reasonable time."

"Get your arse out of bed Hunter, before I send your mother in." Threatened James. "We need to get you back to your old self. Which means back to our old training routine."

Sensing he wasn't going to win this one, Hunter finally got up and dug out some running gear.

"Meet you downstairs in five." James stated, ducking back out.

The sun wouldn't be seen for another hour, but the world was bright with the lightness of the snow. It wasn't too deep, only an inch or two in most places, and it had a thick frost on the surface that was childishly satisfying to crunch through.

It was bloody cold, and Hunter jogged on the spot to try and keep warmth and sensation in his body. James stretched next to him, then stood straight and gave a nod.

The two men set off at a jog – their routine was to keep it steady for a quarter lap of the estate, then kick it up a gear. This morning though, when Hunter would usually be the first to run, he was lagging behind, his breath burning his lungs and an unfamiliar dizziness threatening to take over.

James looked back and slowed a little. "You know, I'm liking being the fastest for once. Makes up for all those times you left me in the dust."

Despite the cheeriness of his voice, it was obvious that James was worried about Hunter. Not just the here and now, but what would happen if the witches attacked while he was like this? James had never gone into a situation without knowing the strong, fast Hunter was beside him.

"Quick break?" Hunter suggested, embarrassed that he needed one already.

James nodded over to the old gatehouse that wasn't far away. The door was unlocked, and soon they were inside the single, simple room. It wasn't warmer inside this old building, but at least they weren't standing in snow for five minutes.

James kept moving with some stretching exercises, waiting for Hunter to carry on the run; to talk; anything.

"This is embarrassing. I've never been this weak." Hunter eventually muttered.

"Yes you have. It's been a year since you were recovering from that coven attack in Wiltshire, remember?"

Hunter paused, he'd been so wrapped up in this near-death experience, he had forgotten about that one. "Oh yes. And then you persuaded me to take a holiday. So, I did, and ended up meeting the Shadow Witch."

"So, I won't recommend a holiday this time." James shrugged.

Hunter flexed his knees, feeling his muscles protest. "I can't believe how unfit I am."

"I can." James replied. "Oh, come on, when was the last time we went running? Ever since you've been shacked up with Sophie, I haven't seen you on a single mornin' run!"

Hunter was surprised at James' outburst and was immediately defensive. He'd had a lot to think about these last few months. Charlotte's murder; the destruction of the MMC; the woman he loved wanting to kill him. But Hunter had to confess that James was right, he'd been too distracted by Sophie, neglecting his friend... but she had been too tempting to tear away from. Not that it mattered now.

"She fooled me too." James said quietly, reading Hunter's thoughts. "Oh, I thought she was a frigid bitch at times, but I trusted her too."

Hunter looked over to his friend. Any response that sprung to mind was pathetically incapable of expressing

23

how foolish he felt. Not that he wanted to get into this right now, or anytime soon.

"Let's get moving." Hunter said, heading back towards the door. "We'll take the shortcut back to the house and do the full lap tomorrow."

James shrugged. "Fine. Then after breakfast we'll practise combat. I'm looking forward to knocking you on your arse for once!"

Chapter Four

Hunter was pleasantly surprised at his rate of recovery. After a week of training, he was as strong as James, and then he started to win some of the spars and was soon running ahead of him once more. The Yorkshireman pretended to be sour over his new losing streak, but he was (not so-) secretly relieved that Hunter was getting back to his old self.

Not only that, but slowly others began to join them in the pre-dawn run, and even more joined the sparring sessions. Witch-hunters and soldiers that were restlessly waiting for this war to progress first came to watch out of curiosity, most of them never having seen Hunter in action. Hunter suspected Marks and Hayworth had encouraged them to participate, and after being initially annoyed at the invasion of his privacy, Hunter welcomed them. They moved the session from the indoor hall to the courtyard as numbers grew.

It quickly became habit that Hunter would drift through the men and women that fought barehanded, or with short poles. He would offer correction and advice where necessary, but on the whole, it was uplifting to see the level of skill.

A couple in particular impressed him. A sergeant from the army, Ian Grimshaw proved unbeatable in hand-to-hand combat, grappling and flooring every opponent. When Hunter spoke to him, Sergeant Grimshaw was a very quiet man in his late thirties, who just happened to turn his hand to martial arts from a young age.

The other was a 3rd gen witch-hunter, Alannah Winton, a petite brunette Welsh girl who was scarily accurate and fast with the poles. When asked about her background, she just grinned mischievously and told them that they should see what she could do with real knives!

Hunter quickly promoted them to step in and help the others, he watched as Ian and Alannah moved through the others with purpose.

Near the end of each session, everyone began to wind down, and stayed to watch Hunter. It had been annoying at first, to have the audience, but Hunter quickly shut them out.

Normally he fought James, but today both Ian and Alannah faced him. All three held the short poles and stood as the three points of a triangle. Ian and Alannah were kitted out with padded vests and gloves, but Hunter shunned the safety equipment. He knew that he was too strong and fast to allow anyone to actually land a hit, he allowed himself to be more than a little arrogant in that respect.

Hunter took a deep breath, letting his shoulders drop down and relax. He felt his usual wave of calm and confidence wash over him; he raised his eyes to look at his opponents, waiting for them to attack.

Alannah was the first to move, and she didn't hold back. For someone so young and standing half a foot shorter than Hunter; she was strong and fast – faster than he expected a 3rd gen to be. She swung her pole at his right side, which Hunter deflected with a resounding crack; then brought her knee up to his exposed left side. Surprised at her dirty move, Hunter barely got his arm in place to stop her. He went to grab her leg, but Alannah read his intention, and pulled back before he could unbalance her.

Before Hunter could recover, there was a blow to his right shoulder. For a man so big and looming, Ian could move bloody quietly – Hunter hadn't even noticed him! Ignoring the spike of pain, Hunter spun round, raising his pole just in time to deflect his second strike. He threw his weight behind the move, pushing Ian back.

Hunter rolled his injured shoulder, and smirked at his own over-confidence. It was going to get him killed one day.

This time they both came at him, Alannah forcing him to block high, while Ian tried to slip past his guard. Hunter grunted as Ian's hastily deflected blow caught a rib. 'Move faster,' Hunter scolded himself.

He twisted away, causing Ian to unbalance, and catching Alannah with a bruising crack on her outstretched arm. Alannah was the first to reach him again, she moved quickly and rattled out a few sharp attacks that Hunter had to focus to parry. The Welsh girl was more than impressive, despite her youth.

Partially distracted by having to stop Alannah knocking his head off, Hunter had momentarily forgotten Ian and was shocked to feel a pair of arms pin around his chest. He struggled against the iron grip – he had seen others unable to break out, but it surprised him that neither could he. He took a deep breath and prepared to throw Ian over his shoulder; he felt Ian's muscles tighten and lock down in anticipation for the move.

Hunter closed his eyes and... and no longer felt the constricting arms around his torso. There were gasps all around, and Hunter opened his eyes to see that he was standing behind Ian...

Hunter glanced around and saw only shock on the faces of the audience. Ian span round, his expression one of confusion, as he looked from his hands to where Hunter now stood.

It finally dawned on Hunter that he had instinctively blinked the short distance to escape the grip. That was useful, but-

"That's cheating, Astley." Anthony Marks stood in front of the crowd, his arms crossed over his chest, as he assessed the other witch-hunter. "But it looks like you're ready for duty. Report to myself and Hayworth when you're finished up here."

Hunter nodded, and watched the older witch-hunter retreat. He turned back to his opponents, who stood a little dazed, and looking a little cheated.

"Ah, no hard feelings guys?" Hunter asked.

Alannah shrugged, pushing her sweaty fringe out of her eyes. Ian stared towards Hunter, but then gave a rare, crooked smile.

"Hey, we're on the same team. Can't wait to see you pull that shit out on the witches."

As Hunter approached the dining room, he thought about knocking, but it seemed ridiculous to knock in his own house, so he walked straight in.

28

General Hayworth was standing in the room with another man that Hunter found familiar.

The General looked up to see Hunter, then turned to speak to the other man. "Sergeant Dawkins, can you send for Marks. And bring the list."

Hunter watched Dawkins leave, suddenly remembering the sergeant that had played the guinea pig when Hunter had been experimenting with transporting himself and others in a blink. The man appeared different now he wasn't looking pale and nauseated.

"Anthony told me you're ready to go?" General Hayworth took a seat at the dining table and motioned for Hunter to join him.

"As ready as I'll ever be, sir." Hunter replied. He found it odd that he should be invited to sit in his own house, but everyone was quickly signing up to the attitude that this was just another base for the MMC, in which Hunter was just another witch-hunter.

The far door opened, and Anthony Marks and Dawkins walked through. Dawkins carried a thick folder, which he promptly set on the table.

"Dawkins, this is your project, so if you wouldn't mind." The General said, opening the floor to his second-in-command.

Dawkins nodded, his hand resting importantly on the folder. "After the fall of your MMC, we've been trying to recover as much data as possible. I've been heading the team in charge of listing MMC employees. This is the most current list of witch-hunters and last known locations."

Dawkins opened the folder and lifted the first few sheets, setting them aside. "These are confirmed fatalities."

Hunter looked at the papers covered in dense writing with morbid curiosity. He didn't really want to concentrate on those they'd lost.

Dawkins took a slightly thicker wedge of papers from the folder. "These are witch-hunters relatively local to Little Hanting. We've already sent teams to attempt contact, with varying success."

The Sergeant tapped the still-considerable stack. "And these are the ones further afield."

"Now that you're up for travelling again, we need to make use of your... talent." The General broke in. "We need real time communication and answers, not wasting fuel on days of travel with no promise of result. You will co-ordinate with Sergeant Dawkins, who will prioritise the most likely locations. You will establish communication protocols with any groups, and bring individuals here. Plus, I want reports on any updates about the witches and their leader."

Hunter sat a little perplexed by his orders. He was a witch-hunter, the MMC sent him targets and he took the necessary actions. He wasn't a soldier, but Hayworth was treating him as one. Maybe that would be a good thing, making the MMC a more controlled, and militarised establishment.

Marks cleared his throat. "We've assigned you a team. Alannah Winton, 3rd gen; Sergeant Grimshaw; and Lieutenant Coulson. You leave tomorrow on your first assignment."

Hunter looked up at Marks. "With permission, sirs, I'd like to include James Bennett in my team."

Marks looked over to Dawkins, questioningly.

The Sergeant stayed quiet for a moment, then shrugged. "I suppose I can spare him from my team. If the famous Hunter Astley insists."

Hunter didn't know how to take Dawkin's comment, but hoped it was misunderstood humour. He was surprised that someone else valued James, when he had only ever been a lowly 1st gen to the MMC. But then Hunter felt guilty for his surprise.

"Is there anything else, gentlemen?" Hunter asked.

After a chorus of 'no', Hunter stood and excused himself.

Chapter Five

The following morning, Hunter met the rest of his team at breakfast. The five of them were quiet and awkward. How did one act when suddenly expected to work with, and put their life in the hands of four strangers?

Hunter glanced over towards Ian. The sergeant was the calmest in the group. But as he was also the oldest, in his late-thirties, Hunter wondered if that had anything to do with it.

Lieutenant Maria Coulson leant against the kitchen top near Ian. Her blonde hair was scraped back into a hasty bun, and her blue eyes were half-closed over her coffee. Hunter hadn't personally met Maria before, but had heard good reviews about her. She was supposed to be one of the best gunmen in General Hayworth's regiment.

James yawned, looking outwardly relaxed as he slumped over the breakfast bar. But Hunter could see his nervous tells as James irritatingly tapped his mug.

Next to James, Alannah was wide-eyed and positively bouncing. When she noticed Hunter looking her way, she grinned.

"It's my first big assignment." She spurted out in her lovely Welsh tones. "I'd just finished training when all this kicked off."

"Who did you train with?" Hunter asked.

"Timothy Jones, near Cardiff." Alannah replied. Tucking loose hair behind her ear. "He's on the missing list, so I'm hoping we get to find him."

"Well, I can talk to Colin Dawkins for ya." James piped up, beside her. "Get him to bump up the priority of Jones."

Alannah turned to James, smiling at his help; just as Hunter rolled his eyes at his friend's chumminess with the sergeant.

"Sorry to interrupt, but when are we going?" Ian suddenly asked, looking over at the three witch-hunters.

Oh yes, the business of the day. Hunter glanced round his team. "Get kitted up and meet me back here in ten minutes."

Hunter checked and re-checked his gear. The black stab-vest was comfortable and familiar, his hands traced over the guns and knives that were MMC issue; finally his hand rested on the ever-present dog tags at his neck. This tarnished accessory wasn't just a memento from the last World War, it had come from the Astley collection and was charmed to protect the wearer from certain spells.

Hunter tucked the dog tags into his shirt and made a detour to the vault that lay beyond the library. Taking a lamp with him into that windowless room, he quickly picked out a few suitable pieces. Hunter made his way to the kitchen where everyone was already waiting for him.

"Here, take these." Hunter handed out a necklace to Alannah; a brooch to Maria; and a bracelet to Ian.

Alannah looked excited, understanding the gift immediately, but the two soldiers looked a little confused.

"Uh, thanks?" Maria replied, turning the bronze brooch with amber stone in her hands.

"They're charmed items for extra protection against witches." James explained with a chuckle. He raised his right hand, showing the thick gold ring that he never went without. "You're part of a select group now. Hunter doesn't openly share his treasures."

Hunter stood quietly by the kitchen door. Since he'd taken charge of Astley Manor and its contents six years ago, he'd only given out a very few of these items. James Bennett and Charlotte King had been the first. Sophie Murphy had been the most recent, Hunter wondered whether she still wore the silver and opal necklace.

"Come on, if everyone is ready, we should go." Hunter closed the topic.

Maria pinned her new brooch onto her shirt, then looked up at Hunter, nervous for the first time. "So... what do we have to do? Set candles? I can't promise to be any good at chanting."

Hunter ignored James who immediately burst into laughter at Maria's naivety.

"No, it's not magic. And not that type of magic – that's casting you're thinking of."

Maria blushed, but remained defensive.

"Well I didn't know. Two months ago, I didn't know witches existed, so give us a break while we catch up." Her eyes narrowed in the direction of James, who was gaining control of his mirth.

"All you have to do is hold onto me, I'll do the rest." Hunter explained calmly. "Close your eyes if you want. It can be a, ah- disorientating experience the first time."

34

"Tell me about it." Ian muttered. He was pale from the mere memory of it, having been part of the regiment Hunter had brought to Little Hanting to face the Shadow Witch.

Hunter sighed and held out his arms. Once he felt four hands gripping him tightly, he closed his eyes and let his mind refocus.

The next moment they were gone.

They reappeared in the middle of a field, the rain pouring relentlessly down and soaking each man and woman to the bone within minutes.

"Right, we're five miles outside of Newcastle, there's a small MMC branch a mile to the East of our location." Hunter stated, looking up to see the Angel of the North to confirm his bearings, but only seeing grey cloud. He hoped he wasn't too far out.

Hunter looked at his team, and was hardly surprised to see the youngest, Alannah, on her knees in the mud trying not to throw up. James hovered next to her, trying to be supportive.

The two soldiers had a little more control, although they looked very pale – but that could just have to do with the rain rather than Hunter's method of travel.

"And we've gotta do that every mission?" Maria gasped, half regretting her promotion to this team.

"There and back." Hunter confirmed. "But don't worry, I'm sure you'll get used to it."

Maria groaned at his lack of helpfulness.

"Well, what are we waiting for?" Ian asked. "Winton, you good?"

Alannah nodded and with James grabbing her hand for support, she got back to her feet.

"Lead the way, sir." Ian turned to Hunter.

Hunter recognised the expression that flickered across the usually cool sergeant's face. It was the same expression that so many wore when first working with Hunter. Doubt. So many people were sceptical of the supposed skill of the 7th gen and questioned his right to lead. Especially when that person was older or more experienced.

Hunter felt his pride flare up. Well, he'd just have to prove to Ian, and anyone else that might question him just why he deserved to lead.

But for now, they had to get out of this rain. It was no fun, trudging across the muddy field, slipping in the harrows and their boots getting heavier with mud and rain. Eventually they hit a road and followed it until it led to the A1. The motorway was eerily quiet, and Hunter and his team jumped across the barriers and walked across the tarmac, the only noise the consistent rain.

On the other side of the main road was their destination. It looked like any other trading estate, with industrial offices standing blandly side by side, and the token car depot. But amongst the boringly normal enterprises here, the MMC had held an office for years.

Hunter led the way to a red-brick building. There was an electronic keypad by the main door, which had been rendered useless along with most other things, when the witches had overturned technology with magic.

But there was a keyhole. Unfortunately, Hunter didn't have the key. He wondered… Hunter focused on the lock, tried to mentally feel out the latch and give it an invisible shove… It felt like it was about to move, but always slipped at the last moment.

From the back of the group, James huffed and pushed to the front.

"Get out the way." He muttered to his friend. Hunter might want to experiment, but James was bored with getting soaked and was impatient to get inside.

James took out his tools for the job and knelt by the door. Less than a minute later there was the rewarding sound of a click, and the door drifted open. James stood back and allowed Hunter to lead the way into a dark corridor.

"Stop there. Identify yourself." A voice came from the far end of the corridor.

Hunter's sharp eyes made out the shape of a person kneeling, a gun in hand. He had no doubt that this person could see them, silhouetted in the doorway.

"We're from the MMC. I'm Hunter Astley, 7th gen."

"Really?" The voice remained wary. "Come to the control room, and we'll see."

A door opened, letting daylight in the far end of the corridor.

Hunter spared his team a quick glance, then led the way down to the door. He stepped into the 'control room', which looked like it had once been the main meeting room for this MMC branch. Now tables had been pushed together and were piled with papers. On the wall were two maps – one local and one national – both had marks and notes covering them.

But more importantly, half a dozen men stood aiming guns at the trespassers.

"Hunter?" One of the men lowered his gun and moved to the front. "James? Christ, I'm glad to see you two!"

"Toby? What on earth are you doing here?" James piped up.

Hunter quickly placed the face. Toby Robson, a 4th gen witch-hunter that had been listed as missing. But they had been searching for him near his home of Oxford, not Newcastle.

"Oh, long story. I was on my way back from a family excursion to Scotland when everything happened. I got stuck here, and well, we've been busy ever since. We had no idea if there were other survivors." Toby replied, his eyes locked on his old friends, savouring the sight of them again. "What about you? I mean, what's the state of the MMC? What happened after the blackout? Hell – what was the blackout?"

"Sir?" Maria piped up from behind Hunter, the soldier looking amused at the flood of questions. "Perhaps we should check the others off our list while you fill your friend in."

Hunter nodded, glad that someone had suggested something sensible. He coughed, wondering where to start for Toby. "So… what do you know?"

An hour later, Alannah was still quizzing the other witch-hunters over what they knew of their colleagues and witches; and the other three members of Hunter's team sifted through the stacked data.

Hunter was sat with Toby, who looked a little dazed at all he had just been told. He'd been sitting like that for nearly ten minutes, and Hunter wondered whether he should speak, or wait patiently for his friend to snap out of it.

Hunter coughed, and less-than-subtly drummed his fingers on the table-top.

Finally, Toby looked up at him. "Sophie, you're sure?"

38

Hunter nodded. "I hoped it was some spell, a charm or possession of some sort. But no, it was her all along. She took great pleasure in ridiculing the trust I put in her."

"But... weren't you-"

"Can we change the topic?" Hunter cut through, before Toby could go any more in-depth. "So, tell me, how did you end up here?"

Toby shrugged, not finding his own story half as interesting. "We took the baby up to see the in-laws. Little Molly is a few months old now; it was her first trip to Scotland to see Claire's side of the family. We were still up there when the mass-breakout occurred. I made sure Claire and Molly were safe, then went to fight at the Glasgow prison.

"It took a few days to help with the casualties and a few sporadic witch attacks. After that, I was determined to get back and report to our MMC, but only got as far as Newcastle when everything blacked out. I came straight here to get answers, but everything was chaos. They'd lost all contact with the head office, and of the witch-hunters that hadn't been killed, many were missing. I stayed to help – I've been here a month now."

"Are you in charge?" Hunter asked. "What have the primary aims been?"

Toby nodded in answer to his first question. "Yes, I'm the highest gen here, and even though I'm not a Geordie, they seem to trust me; and need me. As for what we've been up to – re-establishing links; trying to find lost hunters; trying to get in touch with other survivors and sounding out what the witches are up to."

"Sounds much the same as us." Hunter murmured.

"Do you need me to come back with you?" Toby asked.

Hunter shook his head. "I think you're more useful to the MMC here, doing what you are already doing. As long as you don't mind?"

Toby sighed and leant back in his chair. "I want to go home, but at the same time it's a relief not to. I don't know how I'd cope to see everything in ruins."

Hunter could understand Toby's logic. Didn't they all want to hide from seeing the worst.

*****

Hunter and his team returned to Astley Manor in the early afternoon. They held gingerly onto their leader and allowed him to rip them from one place to another.

They suddenly appeared in the kitchen, startling Sergeant Dawkins so that he dropped his tea. Not that he seemed to care; he smiled openly when he realised who it was, and what it meant.

"Back already? Amazing!" Dawkins glanced over the team, noting their pale faces with a knowing smile. He wouldn't voluntarily travel with Hunter again. "What did you find?"

"The Newcastle branch is still going strong. We managed to check off eighteen names that reported to their commanding officer, Toby Robson. And, ah, twenty-six confirmed dead." Hunter reeled off.

"Very well. Deliver your notes to my team, and I think a successful first mission deserves the rest of the day off. I'll have your next packet ready in the morning." Dawkins replied. "Ah, James. While you're here, could I steal you? I want your opinion on your replacement."

Chapter Six

After their debrief, Hunter left his team and wandered down to the library. The Astley library was famous in witch-hunter circles. It was the most extensive known collection of books, grimoires, and witch-hunter chronicles. All collected over the last two-hundred years by the Astley family.

He picked up the book that he'd left on the desk yesterday: 'Witches and their Hunters of the Romanic Region: 16th Century study'. The cover was old, brown leather; the lettering dull and cracked. It was just one more book amidst a room full of older, and much more interesting books. But this was the one that contained the reference to the mysterious Benandanti.

There was only a little information, barely a page's worth; giving a brief account of their history as defenders of the Friuli region of Italy and their abilities. Oh, and of course, their ultimate prosecution as witches by the MMC.

Hunter had read it enough times to know the words by heart, and now he stared at the cover, as though willing it to divulge more. Hunter sighed and put the book back down. He wondered how Sophie had made such a questionable connection between himself and these Benandanti, from such a small piece of information. Had she found more details somewhere in this library? Or had she been so desperate to find a way to keep Hunter with her, she'd made the mental leap?

Hunter couldn't say which answer made him more hopeful. To know that the information was somewhere within reach was what brought him here so often. But it would also be a relief to know that Sophie had loved him… Oh, logically he could say that the strength of her affections could make her less likely to be able to kill him; but if he was being honest, he just wanted some evidence that she had loved him back.

Hunter shook his head. He had to stop thinking about her. Sophie Murphy was just the human façade of the Shadow Witch, designed to mislead him. That woman was gone, and she was not coming back.

He stalked over to the bookshelves, where James had left a marker for the next in the 'to-read' pile. Researching both his new-found abilities, and an answer to defeating the Shadow Witch would be distraction enough.

Hunter picked up a book by an American scholar, Eliade. Being from only the 1970's it was positively new compared to some of the others in this room. But Hunter was tired of reading and translating the varying spellings of Olde English, at least this would give his brain a break.

Half an hour later he was engrossed in an account of the history of the interaction between the Inquisition and the Benandanti when a shadow crossed into the room.

"Still reading?"

Hunter glanced up to see General Hayworth with his arms crossed in the doorway.

Hunter shrugged, putting a bookmark in place. "I... I need to find out more about what I am."

Hayworth looked down steadily at the younger man. "Hunter... may I make a suggestion? The books will still be here tomorrow. Spend some time with your team, that's just as important."

The General sighed at the stubbornness of this younger generation, then turned and duly left Hunter to his own devices.

Hunter ran his fingers across the spine of the book, not completely convinced. He knew he couldn't settle to read that stodgy material once more – damn Hayworth for breaking his concentration!

Muttering to himself, Hunter extinguished the lights in the library and sloped towards the living room, drawn by the sound of voices and laughter. He opened the door to see his team sitting around the coffee table, fully entertained by a simple pack of cards. And a few bottles of wine.

"What's the celebration?"

Four heads turned in his direction.

"Well, you know, surviving our first mission seemed a good enough excuse." Maria replied with an innocent air.

"Yeah, just to let you know Hunter, you kindly donated the booze." James informed him.

Hunter shrugged. "Fine. I just hope you guys are fit for duty in the morning."

Three of them looked suitably abashed, but James just snorted. "Ignore him – he'll be as rat-arsed as the rest of us by the end of the evening. Ian, deal him in!"

Hunter's smile finally broke through the stern façade. He stopped to grab a spare glass from the sideboard, then joined his team at the table.

"What are we playing?"

"Blackjack." Ian replied, dealing seven cards in Hunter's direction.

Hunter sighed. "Really? Was this James' idea? You won't beat him."

"I might have suggested it." James replied, smirking as he reordered his cards.

Hunter shook his head, but joined the game. He hadn't played this particular card game since university – where James Bennett had taught him all of the rules, and none of the cheats.

The group continued to play, each of them occasionally winning, but James coming out on top most rounds. They steadily drank through the wine that he had raided from the Astley cellar, and chatted away.

Hayworth had been right, in Hunter's opinion, he was learning more about the people he was expected to work with and trust in this one tipsy evening, than he had with weeks of training.

But occasionally a serious question popped up that made Hunter shrink back.

"Why does the Shadow Witch hate you so much?" Alannah asked Hunter, her cheeks flaring red as she dared ask.

Hunter felt a cold soberness stab through the haze. "It's complicated. My grandfather killed her great-grandmother. She blames my family for setting a witchkind revolution back seventy years."

"That the truth?" Ian grunted, as he leant forward to refill his glass.

"What's that supposed to mean?" James snapped, suddenly defensive on his friend's behalf.

Ian shrugged. "Seems a weak reason for that attack the other month."

James grew redder, and Hunter could see the warning signs. He turned to Ian before James could embarrass them. "Yes, it's the truth. The Shadow used my family name as a focus for her anger and revenge. I imagine that has intensified. Not to boast, but being the only 7th gen witch-hunter, she sees me as a major adversary."

Talking about why the Shadow Witch hated him was easy. Hunter was glad that his team was ignorant enough of certain facts, that they did not quiz him over why the same woman loved him. That was a twisted story.

"I'm sorry, I didn't mean to cause upset." Alannah gushed, her cheeks burning red with embarrassment.

Maria chuckled at her side and put down a card on the pile. "Last card."

"Don't worry Ian." James said, throwing three cards down. "We've all joined Hunter on the top of the witches' hitlist, just by associating with him. Pick up five, Hunter."

Hunter groaned at how the game was going. "You are taking the proverbial piss, Mr Bennett. Why can't we play poker instead?"

Alannah put down a single card, pouting at the collection she had amassed. "Only if it's strip poker."

Maria laughed, while Ian groaned. "Nah, if you guys are starting that game, that is my cue to leave."

Maria looked over at her superior, a spark of challenge in her eyes. "Afraid you'll lose, sir?"

"Never! But someone has to maintain decorum and control." Ian replied, in equal jest. "Plus, I don't think my partner would approve of me playing strip anything with you youngsters."

James threw his cards on the table. "I'll start with a handicap, as I'm not gonna lose a round." He said, and before anyone could stop him, he dragged his jumper over his head.

Alannah watched his bare torso with a certain admiration, but Maria only snorted at his actions. "Hey, I was going to win that last game! You did that on purpose."

James very maturely, retaliated by throwing his jumper at her.

Chapter Seven

Over the following week, Hunter and his team fell into a steady pattern. They would run before dawn, then have breakfast together. Then James would bring the latest assignment from Sergeant Dawkins, and off they would go.

One morning, James audibly groaned as he opened the manila containing their assignment.

"Shit, I thought I'd pushed this off onto another team." James muttered, looking warily towards Hunter.

"Who is it?" Maria asked, grinning at his discomfort. James remained silent, passing the document to his team leader.

Hunter took one look at the sheet and swore. "They want us to enlist this git? We are better off without him."

"Ok, you're just teasing now." Alannah chided, trying her best to look disinterested. "Who is it?"

Already bored with the morning banter, Ian moved across the room and snatched the sheets from Hunter. "Gareth Halbrook. Never heard of him."

Maria shrugged, none the wiser. But Alannah sat trying to remember what she knew on the man.

"He's supposed to be good, isn't he? Like, really good. He's a high gen too; 3rd or 4th?"

"4th." Hunter confirmed. "But he's an arse."

"Why?" Maria asked, her blue eyes narrowing in James' direction.

"You'll see." He sighed. "Come on, the sooner we go, the sooner we get this over with."

Maria and Alannah shared a look, curious who could get their witch-hunters so riled up. In contrast, Ian got quietly to his feet, ready for whatever came his way.

Once they all had a firm hold on Hunter's arms, they were pulled into the temporary darkness, before opening their eyes to an empty car park.

Hunter noted how his team looked a little pale, but steady. That was good news, to know that people could get used to his method of transport. He felt the need again, to explore what he was capable of. But this was not the time, nor place.

The place, according to James, was the South side of Leicester. They had blinked into a small car park that was a few streets from Halbrook's house.

Finding no reason to put this off, Hunter sighed. "Let's go."

Ten minutes later, James stuffed the AA roadmap back into his bag, as they traipsed down the street where Halbrook lived. It was deserted, like everywhere else. They had caught a sight of a couple of youths, but they had run away, out of fear no doubt.

Hunter wondered how long it would take for everyone to go back to normal. Or what form would the new normal take?

Hunter was spared having to think about it by their arrival at Halbrook's house. Hunter hammered on the door and waited.

"Sod off!" A yell came from inside.

Hunter threw James a weary look, then knocked again. "Halbrook, open the bloody door!"

There was silence on the other side of the door, followed by the shuffle of feet and the click of a key in the lock. The door opened, and Halbrook showed his face. He didn't look like Hunter remembered; neat enough in appearance, with an over-whelming arrogance. No, now his face was sunken and ashen behind the patchy growth of beard. Even more over-whelming was the stench of stale alcohol, and stale unwashed bodies.

But Halbrook looked at Hunter with and almost reassuring expression of contempt.

"What the hell do you want, Astley?"

"We're here to discuss the Council. Can we come in?" Hunter asked, not keen on entering the house, but aware of the protection it would have.

Halbrook looked over the group that crowded onto his porch, then shrugged. Leaving the door open as a reluctant invitation, he walked back along the hall and into the sitting room. Halbrook opened the curtains to allow a little light into the room; which was helpful because there was all manner of clutter obstructing the path of his visitors.

"Thought the MMC had fallen." Halbrook muttered.

"Yes, and no." Hunter replied. "The headquarters were destroyed, and our forces scattered. But we are re-grouping."

"So, who's in charge, you? You grasping, little-"

"Marks!" Hunter barked, cutting him off. "Anthony Marks is in charge now."

49

Halbrook guffawed at that. "Should'a guessed. You'd never step up and take responsibility boy, you're too busy acting the hero."

Hunter took a deep breath and tried not to rise to Halbrook's tormenting.

Seeing his friend about to lose it, James stepped in. "Mr Halbrook, we need to make a record of-"

"You're still keepin' this pen-pushing 1st gen around?" Halbrook barely spared James a glance. "And what other useless groupies have you brought with you?"

"Sergeant Grimshaw; Lieutenant Coulson; and Alannah Winton, 3rd gen." Hunter reeled off, going down the line.

Halbrook snorted, not impressed. "A measly 3rd gen that looks like she should still be in school, and a couple of grunts from the army – their ranks only distract from the fact they're as incompetent and unprepared as your pet 1st gen."

Hunter felt his anger boiling over, when a quiet voice spoke at his shoulder.

"With your permission, sir?"

Hunter turned to see Ian looking challengingly in Halbrook's direction. He had the sudden flashback of when Ian had fairly bettered him on the training grounds, and he had only gotten away by cheating. The idea of Halbrook getting floored was enough to make Hunter smile, and fight back his mood.

"Maybe another time." Hunter replied calmly.

James coughed, trying to break the atmosphere. "Mr Halbrook, can you tell us about any other witch-hunters? Colleagues? Apprentices?"

"Dead. All dead." Halbrook nearly shouted, then continued in a much quieter and more bitter voice. "I

50

watched my apprentices killed by witches after the black-out. They had us marked, see. Hunted, by orders of the Shadow Witch."

"What?" Alannah gasped.

"Yeah, anyone who met her while she was pretending to be human has been marked. Guess I'm top of her list." Halbrook looked across to Hunter. "Well, maybe second."

"How did you survive?" Hunter asked, trying to bring the conversation back to point. He didn't know how much Halbrook knew or suspected, and he didn't want to find out.

Halbrook shrugged. "The bastards underestimated me. I got away, and stayed holed up here since. Couldn't leave – there was always a witch or two around on watch. But they disappeared a week ago and I haven't seen them since. Makes me wonder what else is important enough to call them away."

"I don't understand, they just let you stay here?" Maria asked. "Why not break in?"

Halbrook looked at the soldier; she had confirmed that she was an idiot. Wasn't the answer obvious? "Witch-hunter houses are kitted out with protective amulets, as MMC standard. No witch can hurt me here. You'd know that if you had done any research into this organisation you've joined."

Maria's pale skin flushed red, but she did her best to remain calm to his taunts. "Actually, I have done the required reading. Less than a year ago, a better witch-hunter than you was killed, his home destroyed. The initial verdict was an attack from a large coven, though it was later confirmed as the work of the Shadow Witch. But perhaps you didn't find the report on Brian Lloyd important."

51

"Ho! This one's got teeth! And maybe a brain in that pretty little head of yours." Halbrook spat, his lip curling back. "You're still damn useless, as far as I'm concerned. Won't have no 1st gens next to me in a fight."

"Ok, enough!" Hunter snapped, defending his team. "I thought the Shadow Witch was injured in the last battle; her lack of involvement in getting rid of you, Mr Halbrook, may well be evidence to support that theory. We must assume that she will recover, though."

"Yeah, which is why we need you to come with us." James added.

Hunter turned to face James, aghast. "I'm not taking him to the Manor."

"We have our orders, Hunter. Lone witch-hunters are to be taken back to base."

Halbrook snorted. "Orders? Astley is flamin' infamous for ignoring orders. Why should he listen to them now?"

"Actually, I agree with Halbrook, for once." Hunter replied, feeling slightly queasy at the very idea of agreeing with an arse like Halbrook.

Ian stepped forward, and clapped Hunter on the shoulder. "Get over yourself Hunter. Let's get back, out of this shit-tip. No offence." He shot the last couple of words to Halbrook.

The older man just grunted.

"Please hold onto Hunter." James directed, as he grabbed his friend's arm. The two women took their cue and held on.

Halbrook stared at them all. "I don't know what sort of namby-pamby New Age crap you're into, but I am not doing a group hug."

Everyone looked at him, and Alannah ducked into James' shoulder to stifle a giggle.

"Just... hold on." Hunter said, holding out his hand.

Gingerly, Halbrook reached out and held Hunter's wrist as loosely as possible.

Before Halbrook had a chance to back away, Hunter blinked them all into the entrance hall of Astley Manor. His team, now fully habituated to the process, remained standing and unfazed.

Halbrook dropped to his knees, his head on the rug as he groaned.

"What... what the hell..." He broke off as he started to retch.

"Oh, not on the rug." Hunter moaned, gritting his teeth as he watched the bastard defile his house. "Ugh, you are cleaning that up."

Maria tilted her head sweetly as she looked at him. "Don't worry, Mr Halbrook. You're only a measly 4th gen. It's not like you can handle this."

Halbrook wiped his mouth with his sleeve. "You-"

"You are in my house now." Hunter broke in. "Which means you will watch your tongue."

At that moment, Sergeant Dawkins emerged from the dining room, drawn by the sound of voices. "Ah, back already?"

"Colin – this is Halbrook, you can deal with him now." James replied, keen to get rid of the responsibility.

The sergeant looked down at the mess of a man at his feet. "Of course, come through to our control room, and we'll get you some water."

Halbrook pushed himself up so that he was standing, albeit unsteadily. "I might need summat stronger than that."

53

Sergeant Dawkins glanced over at James, but gathered from the Yorkshireman's calm expression that this was ordinary behaviour from their newest recruit.

They made their way into the dining room and Hunter followed – not out of any desire to support Halbrook, but rather to know first-hand what Halbrook had to say. It seemed that he was not the only one that was worried, Hunter noticed the concerned looks that passed between Anthony Marks and General Hayworth.

"Dawkins, can you lead the debriefing of Hunter's team, please. Anthony and I will handle this one." The General stated.

If Dawkins had any objection to this, he remained quiet, and dutifully left.

"Mr Halbrook, it's good to see you again." Anthony Marks said coldly. He was well aware of Gareth Halbrook – not only his absolute lack of manners, but his reputation for leading 'shoot first, ask later' operations. He hadn't wanted the difficult witch-hunter in their ranks, but when General Hayworth insisted they enlist the 4th gen, he had to concede that it was probably best they kept Halbrook in line. He could only imagine what trouble he might cause if he were left alone.

"Marks, heard you're the man in charge now." Halbrook replied, dragging out a chair and making himself comfortable.

"I am. Along with General Hayworth." Marks confirmed, giving a small nod in the General's direction.

Halbrook took a brazen look around the grand dining room, his piggy little eyes taking in everything. "Well, I can guess where we are. Not that I was ever invited to the great Astley Manor. Me and ye dad weren't what you'd call friendly." Halbrook looked towards Hunter,

54

explaining the obvious to the stuck-up, entitled little shit. "But is someone gonna explain how I got here?"

Anthony glanced over at Hunter before replying. "It turns out that Hunter has developed certain powers like the Benandanti."

"What's that?" Halbrook huffed.

"Who's that." Marks corrected. "They were a pagan anti-witch cult from Friuli, Italy. In the 16th century they devoted their lives to repelling witches, and became stronger, faster; they could shield from magic and travel in a blink. Who knows what else they could do?"

"And what happened to them?"

Marks looked at little uncomfortable at this question. "They were, ah, discovered by the MMC and punished as witches."

"So, we're going to follow their example?" Halbrook pressed. Hunter couldn't help but wonder if the older guy sounded too cheerful at the prospect.

"No." Marks replied calmly. "Can't you see what an advantage Hunter gives us? Besides, I'd like to think we are a little more educated than the 16th century MMC."

"Perhaps. Or maybe just a little more desperate."

Hunter narrowed his eyes at the odious bastard. "You know, there is a chance I'm a good guy."

Halbrook shrugged, not won over by Hunter's argument, the witch-hunter revelling in the news that the famed and respected Hunter Astley had received a more perfect punishment than Halbrook could have dreamt up.

Then the General finally spoke up. "I don't give a crap about your antiquated MMC prejudices or politics. Hunter has proven himself time and again. In fact, he's the reason we're all here and all still alive and fighting. If you insist on being difficult, I will ask Mr Astley to drop you off to the witches – let them deal with you."

Halbrook tried to maintain his disinterested air, but the General's threat had at least silenced him.

"Mr Halbrook, is there anything you can tell us about the Shadow Witch?" Marks asked, trying to get this interrogation back on track.

"Nowt that you don't already know. Deadly, unstoppable, magic without limits. If you want other details, ask your boy over there."

"And what is that supposed to mean?" Hunter asked coldly.

"Oh, come on, the Shadow Witch – Sophie Murphy." Halbrook guffawed. "The signs were all there, it was bloody obvious. Maybe you were too busy to notice, Astley. Had she blinded you with her charms?"

Hunter stood suddenly, his chair scraping back across the wooden floor.

"Hunter, sit back down." The General ordered. "And Halbrook, we have decided to keep Hunter's past friendship with Sophie Murphy classified. There is nothing to benefit from it going public, but a lot of damage to morale could occur."

"Friendship – my arse!" Halbrook muttered. "And by damage to morale, you mean damage to your golden boy's image."

The General just smiled in response to Halbrook's taunting. "Well, if you can't follow these rules, we're straight back to the 'hand-you-over-to-the-witches' option."

Halbrook crossed his arms and hunched down into his seat, looking a lot more petulant than a man of his age and reputation had a right to. "Fine. Where am I staying?"

"Ah, not here." Hunter was quick to clarify.

"We'll speak to Wardell – she's in charge of accommodating allies. She'll find space for you." Marks replied. Finding space might be easy – finding other lodgers that could put up with Halbrook might prove tricky.

Chapter Eight

"You used to work with Halbrook?"

Hunter was snapped out of his private reverie, and back to the dull, unused warehouse situated in one of Manchester's boroughs. The rain thrummed down on the distant roof. James and Alannah stood staring out of a grey window, and Hunter stood with Maria and Ian beside some silent machinery.

Hunter saw the incredulous look on Maria's face as she voiced her question.

"Not if I could help it." Hunter said with a shrug.

Beside him, Ian grunted, although Hunter could not tell if it was from amusement or disbelief.

"Regardless of the fact that he is a prick, with no social graces; Gareth Halbrook was always too rash, too gun happy." Hunter explained. "He always believed that all witches were evil and must be killed. There were others that thought similarly – but he was the most vocal about it. The MMC is – sorry, was – moving away from considering it all so black and white. Personally, I always strived to capture witches alive."

"Perhaps Halbrook was right." Ian muttered.

Maria shushed him. "You don't mean that!"

"Maybe not." Ian replied. "Look Hunter, I don't blame you for hoping witches can be redeemed, or whatever. I mean, you're one of them now."

There was the thud of Maria's punch to Ian's side, although it came too late to stop her comrade's heresy.

"Don't take this the wrong way, Hunter, it's just that up until a few months ago, witches didn't exist outside storybooks for us. Even with what we've scrabbled to learn about the MMC... it's hard to tell the difference between what you do and magic." Maria kept a steady eye contact with Hunter, she wasn't embarrassed about her ignorance, she was just stating the facts. It was a relief for Hunter to have someone so matter-of-fact.

"It's not magic. It's sort of the opposite. Having seven generations of fighting against magic and witches, I guess I've evolved to oppose them."

"You know that's a weak-arsed argument." Ian replied, looking very unimpressed.

"So, you're basically an anti-witch?" Maria asked, trying to keep a straight face after Ian's interjection.

"Something like that." Hunter replied. "But that's no reason not to trust me."

"Who doesn't trust Hunter?" Alannah piped up defensively. She and James had wandered back to hear the tail end of the conversation.

Maria rolled her eyes, proving that you never outgrew that little expression.

"No one."

"If you want the proof – look at that blinking thing of yours." Ian argued. "We basically put our lives in your hands every time we travel."

59

Hunter stood silently, suddenly touched by the mutual respect in his team after such a short time. He didn't know why these good people trusted him; but he was grateful.

"Sorry to break up this love-in. But they're here." James announced, nodding towards movement in the west side of the open warehouse.

Hunter and the rest of his team turned to face the newcomers, automatically defensive. A small party made their way towards them, six figures in all, each looking alert and wary.

"Astley?" A woman's voice called out.

Hunter moved forward; his hand reflexively touched the dog tags at his throat, but managing to stay away from his gun.

"It's good to finally meet you." A woman stepped forward, holding out her hand. She looked very young, but the creases around her eyes, and the threads of grey in her otherwise black hair made Hunter guess that she was in her forties.

"Nadira Shah, 4th gen."

Hunter shook her hand, feeling slightly embarrassed that he should finally meet Nadira Shah properly. Oh, he'd seen her years ago, when she'd had occasion to visit his father, but this was different.

"Nadira, a pleasure. How are things going in Manchester?"

Nadira paused, considering how to phrase her answer. "We are winning, for now. The interim mayor has accepted our help. The people are starting to build their lives again. We have neighbourhood watches that sweep designated areas and report anything suspicious. Some sort of communication has been established."

60

Hunter listened, impressed with their progress. "And the witches?"

"We've had a few individual confrontations. Nothing that felt orchestrated. But it's only a matter of time before the Shadow looks this way."

Something about the way Nadira said it made her statement very foreboding.

"You know this?" Hunter asked.

"Manchester is the capital of the North. Logic tells me that – after London – Manchester will be her next target." Nadira stated, then glanced uneasily over her shoulder. "But there's also whispers, ones that we would be foolish to ignore."

"What do you mean?" Hunter frowned, worried that they were missing something.

Nadira motioned one of her men forward. "This is Jonathan. He is here to represent his kin."

"His kin?" Hunter felt foolish for echoing Nadira and looked to the man instead. He looked like an ordinary person, but then so did witches and witch-hunters on the surface. Hunter looked a little more closely, then understood.

Over the years, Hunter had noticed that there was a faint residue of magic everywhere. Witch-hunters naturally repelled it; and witches acted as both a source and magnet of it – which they could increase, or hide completely with practise.

Normal people were not aware of these residues, and the magic ignored them. But this man, Jonathan, fell into a different category. The flecks of magic moulded playful to his fingertips and followed each breath in and out. It did not belong to him, but was there to be borrowed.

"You're a wiccan!" Hunter stated, trying to keep the note of accusation out of his voice.

"Very astute, Mr Astley." Jonathan returned, mildly amused at the witch-hunter's reaction. "They told me you would be."

"A wiccan?" Ian's deep voice rang out. Hunter did not have to look to know that his friend was tense with the idea of the unknown.

"Relax." James answered. "It's like a witch without powers... or a human with magic. Something like that."

Jonathan looked as confused by James' description as the rest of those present.

"I am just a normal man. Wicca has been my religion and education, which allows me to access the world around me."

"What I want to know is why you're here?" Hunter asked, surprised that Nadira would bother with a wiccan. Historically, witch-hunters didn't bother about them – they were relatively powerless, not worth seeking as an ally. And if they turned bad, that was a job for the good old police force, not enough of a threat for the MMC to bother stepping in.

Jonathan smiled bitterly, as though reading Hunter's mind. "Let's forego the traditional prejudice, and you and I might just get on."

"I'll reserve judgement for now." Hunter replied, crossing his arms. "It's the best you're going to get."

Nadira tutted in the background. "You are as arrogant as your father, Hunter. Men are such bothersome creatures. Jonathan is here because his coven, and other cousin covens wish to form an alliance with the witch-hunters against the witches."

62

"Wait." Maria spoke up. "I would have thought that wiccans would be on the witches' side. What with it all being magic."

Jonathan shrugged, and shoved his hands into his jeans pockets, looking very normal and non-magical indeed. "It's true that some wiccans have been seduced by the promise of power, they have broken their Rede with us and joined the witches."

"Rede?" Maria interrupted.

Jonathan took a deep breath, and began to recite. "' An Ye Harm None, Do What Ye Will.' It's basically the codes and rules that bind us. Including binding us from doing harm. We are the servants of nature – and nature is very much out of balance. It is our duty to rectify that."

Hunter sighed. "I appreciate your good intentions, but what good does that do us? We're in the middle of a war, and you've already explained that your code binds you from helping."

"There are more ways to help than fighting and killing!" Jonathan returned sharply. "We have methods of communication for simple messages, and spies that have infiltrated witch ranks as wiccan absconders. Both of which you need, I would imagine."

"Oh." Hunter couldn't think how to reply to that.

There was a snicker from James, the Yorkshireman amused and impressed that the wiccan could silence his friend.

Nadira looked similarly amused. "You honestly thought I would waste your time with someone of no use, Hunter?"

"Fine, what do-"

Hunter was interrupted by a sudden and familiar sound. A single gunshot echoed through the warehouse.

Jonathan grunted as the bullet hit and knocked his to the ground.

Hunter shifted closer to the others, throwing up his shield – it was designed to defend against magic, but he had been known to stop a bullet. Once.

There was another resounding shot… this time the bullet hit Hunter's defences in front of his chest. Hunter glanced down at the small lump of metal, but after learning his lesson last time, didn't touch it. He let it fall to the ground.

Movement on the gangway on the far side of the warehouse caught Hunter's eye.

Luckily, it caught Maria's too. Without hesitation, she raised her gun and shot two rounds.

There was a human cry of pain, and the figure slumped.

Hunter nodded to the lieutenant, and they both set off, running in the direction of the attack. The gangway was twenty feet in the air, but Hunter found the metal ladder, going up first. As he drew up to the level, Hunter could hear laboured breathing. He took slow, measured paces, with his gun steady before him. Hunter noticed a spatter of blood by his feet and followed the red trail.

Hunter spotted the gunman, collapsed in a corner, his breathing shallow, and his face already pale and sweating profusely. The man's black jacket and trousers were wet with blood at the shoulder, and thigh. The man's eyes widened with fear as he spotted Hunter, and he made a weak attempt to raise his gun. Hunter knocked his slow movement aside with his usual speed and dexterity. The gun clattered across the metal gangway.

Hunter heard Maria's light tread behind him. "Let's get him down to the others."

"Yes sir." Maria replied automatically. Then frowned. "How are we going to get him down? I mean, I'm not averse to throwing him over the edge…"

Hunter snorted without humour. Not wasting words, he knelt down and touched the man's shoulder.

A moment later they were back in the midst of the group. The gunman was ash white, but Hunter could only guess whether it was the travelling, or the blood loss that was the cause.

Across the warehouse, Hunter could faintly hear Maria swearing, and clanging back down the metal staircase as she was left to take the slow route.

"I thought you guys could detect witches." Jonathan muttered as soon as he got over his shock at seeing two people materialise in front of him. The wiccan sat on the floor, his shoulder being strapped with a makeshift bandage, by the ever-practical Ian.

"We detect magic, not witches." Hunter clarified. "We can't feel anything out of the ordinary, unless they start casting."

"Oh fantastic!" Jonathan groaned. "I'll remember that excuse later."

Hunter frowned but looked down at the bleeding gunman at his feet. "Anyone you recognise, Nadira? Jonathan?"

"No." Jonathan replied with a sharp hiss as Ian tied off the bandage.

"Well someone has given our position away." Hunter said, looking down at the gunman.

"What do we do with him, boss?" Ian stood, having finished his first aid, and nodded to the now-unconscious man on the floor. "Cos if we continue this chit-chat, he's gonna be dead anyway."

"Kill him." James said, uncharacteristically cold.

"James!" Alannah snapped, grasping his arm.

"Think about it: a single witch gunman was sent to take out a wiccan. If they had known Hunter was involved, it would have been a dozen at least. But all we've gotta do is let him live and get word back to his boss that a witch-hunter could stop his bullets and travel in a blink – how long do you think it will take them to work out Hunter was here? Then what – they come in force to Manchester, and Nadira and her followers suffer."

"Ok, you've been spending too much time with Halbrook." Alannah accused, her green eyes narrowing at James. "What you need to do is take him back to base for questioning."

Ian coughed to get their attention. "Too late. He's gone."

They all stopped, and looked at the gunman, pale and lifeless at their feet.

Chapter Nine

Nadira escorted Hunter and his team back to their base. Two of her men helped Jonathan, who was pale, but insisted on walking back.

Soon they were all settled in a grey and dull office.

"Jonathan will be back after the doctors have seen him." Nadira stood by the door, her arms folded. "Today did not go how I expected."

Hunter pulled out a chair and got comfortable for a possibly long wait. "I doubt it's your fault, Nadira. But we should look into who might have betrayed you."

Nadira stared straight into one of the grey walls, her lips down-turned. She took a minute to process the particulars, then shook her head. "It would have been someone with only partial information. As your man pointed out, they did not know it was you we were meeting."

Nadira sighed. "I almost wish it were someone in my immediate circle of advisors, they are limited in number. But to search for a possible mole in the hundreds of allies here... this war may be over before they are discovered."

"With any luck, this will be over quickly." Hunter replied.

Nadira bit back a smile. "You are too optimistic, Hunter. You remind me of Young, he was the same. Now, I shall see about getting tea."

The woman left Hunter and his team, but was back before they could cause much mischief. This time Nadira brought company into the office.

Jonathan came in, his bloody clothes changed and a fresh white bandage acting as a sling for his left arm. Another witch-hunter followed behind him, carrying a box, which he set on the table.

"How is your arm, Jonathan?" Ian asked.

"It's fine, thank you, Sergeant. No major damage." The wiccan replied. He looked very pale still, but determined to finish this meeting. He nodded to the box. "If one of you could do the honours, please."

Alannah, who was closest to the box, opened the lid. Inside there were at least a dozen smaller boxes about four inches wide. Glancing up to Jonathan, to make sure she had permission, she picked up one of the small boxes and opened it. Inside, on a bed of paper, were two rose coloured stones.

Hunter leant across the table, trying to see what it was. "Is that-?"

"Quartz." Jonathan answered. "Those ones are rose quartz, to be precise."

"What are they for?" Maria asked, looking down at the unimpressive stones.

"We use them for basic communication." Jonathan explained. "These two stones have been cut from the same piece, and have been charmed to interact with each other. If you would pass me one, please, Miss...?"

"Alannah Winton." The Welsh girl offered her name readily, and passed one of the small pinkish stones to Jonathan.

"Thank you, Alannah." Jonathan smiled. "If you would hold the other one."

Alannah grinned as she took up the second stone, it was cool and smooth in her palm.

Jonathan smiled at her cooperation. "So far we have been using these to warn of emergencies. The stones stay connected, no matter the distance. And if I run into trouble and need back-up, I simply focus on the stone…"

Jonathan shut his eyes, and closed his fist over the small stone. After a minute of concentration, Alannah yelped, dropping her stone on the table with a clatter. "It got hot!" She exclaimed, looking at the wiccan for an explanation.

"Not enough to burn, or do damage, but enough to get attention." Jonathan turned the cool rose quartz over in his hand.

Hunter looked on, wondering if he was supposed to be impressed.

"When you mentioned basic communication, I did not realise you meant this basic."

Jonathan did not look fazed by the witch-hunter's apathy. "You are letting yourself be blinded to its usefulness, Mr Astley. If I sent a distress signal, how quickly could you get to me? Opposed to how long it would take for a message of trouble to come via mundane means – providing there's someone able to get that message out, of course."

Jonathan handed his stone back to Alannah, and indicated that she should put them back in the box. The Wiccan waved his good hand at the collection. "Quartz is a powerful magical amplifier, long used for communication. We've just adapted it to suit our needs. There's rose quartz, citrine and amethyst in there, they won't fail you. The stones are reservoirs for magic, once charged they won't run out."

"Isn't quartz the stuff they use in crystal balls?" James asked, reserving some scepticism still.

Jonathan sighed. "That's a different type of magic. But yes. Not that I hold with that type of thing."

"You mean, there are prejudices within Wicca to different types of magic?" James was positively intrigued by the idea.

Jonathan shrugged. "It tends to change with each generation. Whereas clairvoyance was all the rage ten years ago, a lot of us now are taking a more traditional route. Although I hear there's a Boston movement-"

"As interesting as this is, can we please focus?" Hunter interrupted. He got the feeling that Jonathan would prattle on about his religion for as long as James wanted to listen. And Hunter recognised that light of interest in his friend's eyes. They could be there all day. "Let us say that the stones work, and prove useful, there are only a dozen or so here. We would need a lot more if we intended to make it part of every team's essential kit."

Jonathan nodded. "They will work. These are all we can spare, at the moment. My coven needs to wait until the next full moon before we can charm any more. You can pick up the next batch in a few weeks' time."

Chapter Ten

Summer was starting to break out over the English countryside in its usual sporadic fashion. The rain grew warmer, and the grass would grow. The sun would shine promisingly for a day or too, before the grey clouds would roll in again.

The situation was relatively stable, with steady reports finding their way to Astley Manor. Jonathan's communication stones had been implemented with reasonable success, although they hadn't yet been put into practise in an emergency.

Because of the quietness, Hunter had secured home-leave for his team for a week. Using his talents actually felt good when he was blinking to Brecon to reunite Alannah with the rest of her family and taking Ian back to his home in Bristol. When Hunter and James blinked to Doncaster, Hunter had to stay for dinner with his aunt and uncle, and had to suffer the incessant chatter of James' younger cousins.

Back at Astley Manor, there was only one team member left.

Maria was just finishing washing the pots from her lonely dinner, when Hunter walked into the kitchen.

"How were James and the family?" She asked, grabbing a tea towel from the rail.

"Loud." Hunter replied, grabbing a warm beer from the pantry. "Were you alright, eating alone?"

Maria paused with her drying, then shrugged. "It was kinda nice to have some time to myself. I half expected one of Dawkin's team to come in and cadge a meal – it's what usually happens."

Hunter nodded, he understood that the Manor had turned into a hive of activity. He enjoyed it for the most part, filling this big old house with noise and movement. But occasionally it was necessary to find a quiet corner to oneself.

"Are you sure you don't want to go home this week?" Hunter asked.

"Home. It doesn't mean much to me." Maria replied with a sigh. "No mum. Dad died when I was nineteen – just after I joined the army. I married young, then the git left me when I was promoted before him."

Hunter inwardly winced at her casualness. "I'm sorry." He murmured, knowing that it was a largely ineffective comment.

Maria shook her head. "It's fine, it's life."

"Well, I could take you to visit friends instead." Hunter offered.

Maria chuckled at his obvious attempt at cheering her up. She didn't need it; she was content with her life now. "The only friends I have are in the unit stationed here. Thanks for the concern, but I'll spend my free time catching up with them in Little Hanting."

Maria tossed down the tea towel and copied her boss, by grabbing a bottle of beer.

"So, I've shared, now it's your turn." Maria locked her blue eyes on Hunter.

Hunter returned her gaze, feeling a little uneasy. "Ok…"

"Why is the Shadow Witch obsessed with you?"

Hunter frowned and shook his head. "We've been over that already. I'm-"

"Yeah, yeah, you're a major threat and your families have history." Maria interrupted. "I don't buy it, and neither do the others."

Hunter leant back against the hard kitchen work top and took his time to drink his beer.

"Oh, come on, Hunter!" Maria snapped. "We have a right to know – haven't we proven that you can trust us?"

Hunter sighed and idly picked at the label on his bottle. "I do trust you, it's just that Sophie… When I met the Shadow Witch, she was pretending to be human. I saved her from a fake sacrifice, then I helped her join the Malleus Maleficarum Council. So, it's my fault she learned so much inside information."

Maria listened quietly, a little frown forming between her brows as she took in what Hunter shared. "But that doesn't explain why she's focused on you."

Hunter shrugged, thinking back to last summer. "Sophie came to train with me, she came to live here. I thought she was someone I could trust. She was smart, beautiful… a little cold, I'll admit."

Maria's eyes widened as she realised where Hunter was going. "You and the witch?" She asked breathlessly.

Hunter twisted the bottle in his hands, unable to say anything. He knew if he confessed this to another witch-hunter he would be met with disgust. But Maria was new to this fight, she didn't have years of prejudice behind her – or so he hoped.

"Does anyone else know?" Maria asked.

"James – he knew Sophie too. But General Hayworth and Anthony Marks know some details, and I think they have filled in the rest."

Maria chewed over this, then finally looked at Hunter. "Thanks for confiding in me. But Hunter, you should really think about telling Ian and Alannah."

With a sorry smile, Maria ducked into the pantry to grab another beer, then took the bottle and headed to the room she had been allocated.

Chapter Eleven

One pleasant summer's evening, Hunter walked in the gardens of the estate. The flowerbeds of Astley Manor had once been strictly cultivated to Mrs Astley's design. But the two ground-staff and full-time gardener that the family employed had been evacuated with the rest of the village six months ago and had not yet returned.

In those six months, nature had taken control of the garden, and personally, Hunter thought it looked better for it. There was one small corner where his mother actually got her hands dirty and tried to maintain a few flower beds. It was amusing to watch her narrow and focused attempt.

Spoiling the peace, Hunter felt suddenly alert, a flash of pain as he recognised magic in use. It was close, a few miles at the most. Hunter closed his eyes and focused on it – there were two different rhythms - two witches casting, and from his experience, the magic seemed weak.

Hunter sighed, why would such weak witches cast anywhere near the famous Astley Manor – they were asking to be destroyed. Unless it was a trap; and they the bait to the bloody thirsty witch-hunters.

Hunter cursed to himself that his quiet evening was ruined. He glanced about the beautiful grounds, taking a last deep breath of the scented breeze, he turned back to the house.

Hunter had only just opened the front door and stepped into the entrance hall, when he looked up to see his team already mobilising, thanks to Alannah. Her senses might not be as developed as his, but it was useful having another higher gen witch-hunter around.

"Ian, can you get us some back-up?" Hunter requested.

The sergeant nodded and left.

"Big threat?" James asked.

Hunter shrugged as he pulled on his stab vest. "Minor. Too minor, it might be an ambush."

Hunter gave directions to the soldier that would follow on foot, and when Ian returned, they took the quicker route.

The five of them appeared near the lake on the south side of the Manor. The setting sun cast the beauty spot in reds and purples, glinting off the rippling surface of the lake; the manmade dock and benches softened by shadows.

Hunter felt the unsteady throb of magic, and silently motioned for the other four to follow him. Guns ready, they made their way along the shoreline until they reached a copse of trees. Voices came out, too quick and quiet to decipher.

Hunter stepped forward with care and precision, not making a sound in his advance. When he pushed through the last barrier of foliage, what he saw made him halt.

There were six young people – the oldest could not have been older than seventeen, and the youngest looked barely fourteen.

"What the-?" Ian said, stepping up beside him.

The teenagers turned at his voice, and those that had been casting threw spells in their direction.

Hunter drew his shield up, the magic breaking uselessly against it – it was hardly worth the effort, Hunter was convinced their magic was so weak, the talismans his people wore would protect them fully. The shield dropped, but Hunter remained alert for any witches waiting in the shadows to ambush them. But he found it hard to believe that any person could use children as bait – even the witchkind.

"What are you guys doing here?" Hunter demanded.

One rather cocky-looking lad stepped forward as self-appointed spokesperson. "Aren't you meant to give that Malleus speech when addressing witches?"

Hunter paused. This was a new situation. "I save it for the adult witches. Why, do you want me to say it?"

"No." The youth replied immediately, a blush creeping up his neck that he was speaking with the Astley; and because he would never admit that he wanted to hear it.

Hunter sighed. "Fine. By the Malleus Constitution you will surrender now to my authority to be bound and registered. If you refuse to come quietly, I am empowered to take any means necessary."

The youths' reaction was easy to see, they all stood straighter, defiance in their eyes.

"So, go home." Hunter ordered.

The leader looked dismayed. "But-"

"No." Hunter interrupted. "This isn't your fight, so go home to your families."

A girl pushed forward, raising her rather spotty face to look up at the big bad hunter. "We don't have no family. You killed them."

77

"What?"

The boy put his hand out protectively towards the girl. "Yeah, last winter – you killed Jodie, Missy and Mark's parents at the Midlands prison. Then me, Lucretia and Tommy – you killed ours in that little village place."

"Little Hanting." One of the kids backed him up.

"Yeah, there."

Hunter had to stop himself from stepping back. He'd killed people, of course he had, but he never liked associating those people with a life and loved ones. Even if the people were witches, and their loved ones were obnoxious children.

James read his friend's hesitation and stepped in before anyone else noticed. "Ok, so are you gonna explain how that brings you 'ere? Because you have two options – you can surrender and be bound; or you can piss off."

"Or we can kill you!" The leader shouted, riled up by their dismissal. "We out-number you!"

"Not going to happen, kid." Ian stated calmly, crossing his arms and staring the youth down.

The boy tried to keep eye contact, but quickly dropped it.

"Last chance, go home, or we'll be forced to subdue and bind you." Hunter warned, silently wondering if any of his team had brought the necessary items to carry out a binding. Personally, he might have one amulet and silk in one of his many pockets, but since the rebellion, things had turned violent. Hunter's first instinct was no longer to bind a witch – a worrying acknowledgement.

"We ain't afraid of you." The spotty girl snapped.

"You should be." Alannah answered. "Maybe not of Hunter, he's the good guy. But definitely the rest of us."

She pulled out one of her knives, turning it in clear view of the group. "Ian's been known to wrench the odd limb from its socket; Maria will shoot you between the eyes before you can even begin to cast; and James – you don't want to know what he's been accused of."

Her lovey Welsh voice grew colder as she spoke, and as she carried on the teenagers' resolution began to waver. They exchanged worried glances.

Noticing his friends' loss in confidence, the leader turned back to the witch-hunters, furiously pulling a spell together.

Hunter felt the build-up – raw emotion giving it more strength but less stability. He threw up his shield just in time to block the magic as the youth released it. The magic exploded against his shield and bounced back, knocking the boy and his friends flat on their backs.

They scrambled up quickly enough, nothing hurt save their egos.

"Go home and learn what you're doing before you challenge us." Hunter insisted.

The leader stepped forward again, but the spotty girl and another gangly lad grabbed his arms and pulled him back. With an awful lot of noise and pushing, the group made a hasty retreat.

"You've got to admire their courage." Alannah remarked, returning her knife to her belt.

"I can't believe how scary you are for a short person." James remarked. "But what on earth were you about to accuse me of?"

Alannah flashed him a smile. "Best you don't know." She purred.

Hunter ignored their banter and the laughter that followed, he turned to lead his group back out into the open. It troubled him that –

"Stop it right there, Hunter." Maria warned as she hurried to walk beside him.

"Stop what?" Hunter hesitated in his stride, wondering what was wrong.

"You – worrying about those kids." Maria explained.

"But how…?"

"You were looking all pensive." Maria said with a shrug. "We don't need you moping again."

Her dry statement made Hunter smile. "It's just… they are so young. Too young to be in this fight."

Maria glanced over her shoulder at the other three members of the team; Ian walked along silently, while James and Alannah still joked at the back. It was a good team, they were all in their prime, and the best at what they did.

"How old were you when you started being a witch-hunter?" Maria suddenly asked him.

Hunter paused, knowing where this was going. "I was twenty."

Maria rolled her eyes. "Sure, you just turned twenty and suddenly you're a witch-hunter. When did you start training?"

"Actually, physically training – probably about thirteen."

"And I bet you were just itching to start earlier than that." Maria pressed her advantage. "I mean, my dad always told me how I was playing soldiers with the local boys when I was five years old."

Much to Hunter's relief, their conversation was drawn to a close by the arrival of twenty soldiers on the scene.

Hunter greeted the lieutenant in charge. "False alarm. Just a few weak witches that didn't realise where they were – when they did, they scarpered."

The lieutenant looked ill-at-ease. "Shall we track them down, sir?"

Hunter shook his head. "No, they are not worth our effort."

"But sir, our orders are to capture or kill any witches found." The lieutenant stated boldly. "Even 'weak' ones may have information."

"I said no, lieutenant." Hunter snapped. "I will report this incident directly to the General, he will agree with my decision."

Hunter wasn't entirely convinced of his argument. General Hayworth was a decent man, and there was a good level of mutual respect between them, but what if he disapproved of letting the youths go...

Oh well, what was the worst that could happen – they could hardly kick him out of the headquarters and his own house. And putting any kind of restraint on him was impossible, he could blink out of any attempt of confinement. Not that he thought it would resort to such things.

His team shifted closer to him, anticipating that they would travel with Hunter now that business was finished. But Hunter gave a minute shake of his head, and they stopped in place. His team might prefer the quick route home, but Hunter thought it advisable to walk back with the extra soldiers, in case any of them disobeyed, or if any of the kids were foolish enough to come back.

Falling into an unhurried march, Hunter found Alannah next to him.

"Well done for, you know..." Hunter trailed off.

"Dim prob." Alannah replied. "I'm always happy to scare and intimidate."

Hunter smiled as he looked down at the youngest and least intimidating member of the team.

"I can understand why they wanted to fight." Alannah continued. "A few years ago, I was that foolhardy, though I knew it all and that I was invincible. I got into a few scrapes, but I was lucky – Timothy Jones pulled me out of the worst of it and trained me properly. That desire to fight doesn't leave you, though."

"I blame Harry Potter." James piped up as he jogged on to catch up with them. At their disapproving glares, he pressed his point. "No, really, a bunch of pubescent witches and wizards defy and destroy the bad guy."

Hunter marched along; he supposed the comparison made some sense. "So, does that make me Voldemort?"

"Sure." Alannah replied, warming to the theme.

"You've got the looks for it." James added.

Hunter raised his hand to his thick black hair, which honestly needed a cut. "I assume you mean the Tom Riddle phase?"

"Nah."

"Does that make us your Death Eaters?" Ian asked, breaking his usual silence.

"And what does that make Sophie?" Maria added.

"Dumbledore?" James ventured, making everyone laugh.

"Ew, no." Alannah squirmed. "Because that means they, you know..."

"Well, Dumbledore was gay." Ian answered.

There was a pause, before everybody laughed together. A few of the soldiers marching ahead turned to look back and see what the noise was about. Hunter coughed and looked to his team.

Chapter Twelve

One night in the middle of August, Hunter found himself unable to sleep. It could have just been the summer heat that made it uncomfortable, but he felt something foreboding nagging at his senses.

Finally, he dragged himself out of bed, and padded barefoot downstairs to the library. It quickly became a habit now, that when he did not know what to do, he headed to the library in the hope that the next book would yield answers to his problems.

There had been a few hints from his research, but nothing solid. That the Benandanti could walk through dreams, that they could control the elements and manipulate the world around them. But no one mentioned how. He supposed only a desperate and heretical witch-hunter like himself would wish to know the dynamics.

As he entered the library, he tried for the umpteenth time to spark a little life and light in the now defunct light bulb. It wasn't much, to heat the tungsten by exciting the atoms. But no matter how logically he broke it down, Hunter couldn't make the slightest difference.

He thought back to the first time he had transported himself, the first time he had used his shield. It had all happened so easily then, so why was it so hard now? Did he honestly have to wait for his life to be endangered before he unlocked more powers? Or was this it?

Hunter moved to settle down to do more reading but froze. It was so faint, that at first, he thought it was his sleep-deprived imagination. But no, there was the familiar pain that radiated through his brain. Someone was using magic. Hunter got to his feet and focused on it. The source was fifteen miles to the North, only just within range for him to detect.

Before he could even think of getting a team together and investigating, Hunter worked out why this felt so odd. Fifteen miles. He remembered talking to Sophie in this very library, about how a witch-hunter perceives magic. About how he could detect further than the lesser generations. And how far had they agreed he could sense magic?

This was for him. Someone wanted him alone to know that they were there. Before common sense got the better of him, Hunter took a deep breath and focused on the site of the source.

One moment he was in the library. The next he was in the woods that stretched most of the way between Little Hanting and the nearest town.

"Sophie?" He called out, stepping forward. Hunter stopped abruptly, feeling the dewy grass beneath his feet. Barefoot again, damn it. He glanced down to confirm that he was still in his scruffy grey pyjamas.

"Sophie's not here." A familiar voice called back, as a figure stepped forward.

Tall and willowy like her daughter, with the same dark brown hair. Beverley Murphy.

"Bev? What are you doing here? Is Sophie alright?" Hunter rattled off before he could help himself.

In the darkness Bev smiled, her assumptions correct on how this man still felt about her daughter.

"She's fine, Hunter." Bev replied. "I'm here to pass on a message: yesterday she gave birth to a healthy baby boy."

Hunter was struck silent, and after a minute he reminded himself to breathe. He had known that Sophie was pregnant, had known that this day would come. But it was still a shock. He was a father.

"A boy?" He repeated, unable to bring together a more coherent sentence.

"Yes." Bev smiled at the thought of her first grandchild. "Sophie named him Adam."

"Adam?"

"You didn't expect her to call him George, did you?" Bev gave him a shrewd look. "Sophie has had trouble enough hiding the fact that you're the father."

Hunter frowned at this information. "The witches don't know?"

Bev glanced away into the dark woods. "The few that do know decided that it was best the truth was hidden. They don't want the masses to know that their heroic Shadow Witch might have formed an emotional bond with their enemy."

"Sounds familiar." Hunter muttered. Then his eyes narrowed in Bev's direction. "Sophie took a risk sending you, I could have killed you. Why didn't she come herself?"

Bev crossed her arms defensively. "Sophie gave birth yesterday, she's at home recuperating with her new-born son. I was the obvious choice of messenger – you know me, and I, well…"

"You helped me and James escape." Hunter finished, knowing that Bev was telling the truth. She was the one witch he would be willing to listen to. "Thank you, by the way."

Bev shrugged off his thanks. "And Sophie wanted me to… renew her offer."

"The offer where I switch to the side that was willing to kill my best friend?" Hunter returned.

"If you joined us, what is left of the witch-hunters would crumble and yield. You could end this war; you could save so many lives." Bev near begged.

"Do you really believe that I am that important?" Hunter demanded. "Each and every witch-hunter is driven by their own desire to do what is right and good. I could disappear tomorrow, and they would still fight on."

Bev remained silent, as though she had expected this reaction, even as she hoped for better.

Hunter took a deep, calming breath. "If Sophie's so desperate to join forces, tell her to bring a white flag and re-join the MMC."

Bev tutted at the younger man's suggestion. "As if they would accept her. You have more in common with witches than she has with the witch-hunters."

The scene fell silent, Hunter and Bev stood facing each other without speaking as another long minute dragged on.

Eventually, Bev was the one to break the silence. "If there is nothing else, I should be getting home."

Hunter realised that if he had any true conviction, he should stop her, apprehend her for witch-craft, kill if necessary. But instead he just nodded.

"Is there any message you would like me to pass on to my daughter?" Bev asked.

"Tell her... tell her that I..." Hunter grimaced as he broke off. "Never mind. Goodbye Bev."

Before he could break and show emotion, Hunter blinked back to the Manor.

Leaving Bev in the woods. The sound of a sob broke through the night air. Beverley turned to the sound, to find her daughter behind one of the trees.

"I told you not to stay, my darling." Bev said in a hushed voice.

Sophie tilted her head back, taking deep breaths to restore her calm. She brushed the tears from her cheeks, then held her hand out to her mother. Her hazel eyes burnt all the brighter, and they too were gone.

Chapter Thirteen

Hunter blinked back to the library, hoping that way no one would notice his absence. But as he made his way upstairs, the house was quiet and his caution unnecessary.

Instead of heading for his own room, Hunter stopped at James' and knocked on the door. Hunter leant against the doorframe, waiting for James to get his arse out of bed, and was surprised to hear muffled voices from the room.

A minute later, the door cracked open and James' head popped round. He squinted in the bad light until he recognised his friends.

"Oh Hunter, it's you. What's up?"

"I was hoping we could talk."

"What, now? It must be two in the mornin'." James grumbled, then sighed resignedly. "Fine, what is it?"

"Let's go downstairs, I think I need a drink. Plus, it's kind of private." Hunter said, pointedly looking at the door and whoever James was trying to hide behind it.

"Alright, let me just... let me put summat on." James replied, then shut the door in Hunter's face.

Hunter could hear voices and movement, and then the door opened, and James was back.

Despite being plagued by thoughts of tonight, Hunter smirked as James tightened the tie on his robe.

"What?" The Yorkshireman demanded.

Then the door opened behind him and a familiar figure shuffled out, half asleep, and with a white guest robe about her.

"Maria?" Hunter started.

"Ugh, now you've woke me up, I need the loo." Maria muttered. "Don't keep James all night."

Hunter watched in silence as the blonde woman padded barefoot down the corridor to the nearest bathroom.

"I'm surprised, that's not who I expected to come out." Hunter admitted.

"What?" James repeated.

"Well, you and Alannah always seemed so chummy, I thought…"

James frowned. "Alannah? Nah, we're just friends. Come on, I thought you wanted a drink?"

Before Hunter could interrogate him on his love life and further, James led the way downstairs to the drawing room. Once inside, Hunter made a beeline for the drink's cabinet.

"Whisky?" James warily watched Hunter pour healthy measures into two glasses. "This must be serious."

Hunter handed his friend a glass, then jumped straight in before he could lose his nerve. "I have a son. Sophie gave birth yesterday."

James stood there, holding his drink half-way to his lips. A minute dragged by until he was able to speak.

"Con…gratulations?" The single word rose in pitch. James coughed and tried again. "Are you alright, Hunter?"

Hunter shrugged and tilted the golden liquid in his glass. "I don't know. I mean, I knew the day would come."

"What will you do about it?" James asked, sitting on one of the armchairs.

Hunter let out a groan. "What should I do? I can't reconcile things with Sophie. I can't take a new-born baby from its mother. So where does that leave me?"

James shrugged helpfully. "Carrying on as before? It might be a terrible thing to suggest, but Sophie isn't going to hurt him. Maybe… let's finish this thing, then we can concentrate on getting your son."

Hunter drummed his fingers against the glass. "You know what else this means – Sophie is going to step back into the fray, and things are going to get worse."

"You know this?" James asked sceptically.

"It's an educated guess." Hunter countered. "It has been my suspicion that the absence of the Shadow Witch has been due to her pregnancy, rather than any injury gained from the last battle."

James exhaled. "You're gonna have to tell Hayworth and Marks. Even if you don't share all the facts, they need to know to expect a backlash."

*****

After speaking with James, Hunter returned to bed, but tossed and turned and didn't sleep. Eventually when he felt dawn arriving, he could stop pretending and get up.

Pulling on his trainers, he headed out running alone – no one else was mad enough to be up and running before six in the morning. He ran harder and faster than normal, pushing his muscles to the limit, and feeling the sweet distraction of his breathing becoming more rugged and his heart pounding in his chest. Hunter lapped the estate twice, then put in a third at a more leisurely pace to bring

91

his vitals back to normal. But he was still filled with an electric energy. He wasted some more time with a cold bath, then made his way to the kitchen, hoping to catch his boss.

Eventually General Hayworth padded in, looking half-asleep and in the search for caffeine.

"Sir, could I have a word, please."

Taking the General's silence as permission, Hunter took a deep breath and began to explain his theory that the Shadow Witch had only been delayed by pregnancy, and that her return was imminent.

Hayworth stood silently listening to him, giving the odd grunt when he thought Hunter was being less than honest in his account.

"And who told you this?" He barked. "The Shadow's flying monkey?"

"No, her mother." Hunter replied quickly.

"Why would…" Hayworth trailed off as he quickly put the pieces together. "You know what, I don't want to know. So, have you got any theories on where and how, she will strike?"

Hunter sighed, glad that he had gotten the General on side. Or at least as much as Hayworth could be. "Nadira Shah's intelligence points to an attack on the capital. This is backed up with the suspicions of other allies."

The General took this in, then finally nodded. "Right, we'll deploy extra men to London. Dawkins can lead this op."

"Sir, I really think that I-" Hunter started to protest.

"You are too valuable to be stuck in one place, organising troops." Hayworth countered, guessing where Hunter was heading. "You will continue your duties here.

Then, if Dawkins sends a distress signal, you will join the fight. Understood?"

Hunter's shoulders dropped, feeling very much like a castigated child. "Yes sir."

Chapter Fourteen

Little Hanting seemed very quiet indeed after the upheaval of its military residents. They left one gloomy autumn morning, packed into the vehicles they had spent the last few months salvaging, and coaxing into life.

Hunter saw them off, then returned to the Manor.

The next few days felt strange, as Hunter went about his daily routine. When he went running in the morning, only his own team accompanied him; and when he trained after breakfast, less than a dozen joined him in the courtyard. Any less, and they could move the training sessions back inside, like they had at the beginning of the year.

Another week went past, and no news came from London or Manchester. Hunter knew that he was not alone in wishing that the witches would get their attack over with. Wherever they hit, he would take the remaining forces to bolster numbers. Staying at home waiting was getting tedious.

Then one evening, dusk was settling over Astley Manor, the beauty of the sunset lost behind thick clouds. When there was a crescendo of magic that nearly deafened

Hunter. Before stopping to think, he jumped out of his seat and sprinted to the control room.

"Attack!" He shouted, barging into his former dining room.

The control room was already a hive of activity, as people boxed files, and hurried about.

"Yes, Marks felt it too." Hayworth snapped. "Get outside, scout numbers and location. You are not permitted to engage the enemy."

Hunter nodded, and pausing only to arm himself, he left through the front door.

Rain was just beginning to fall, and the heavy cloud and low light would help him to remain invisible. Hunter only hoped his eyes were sharp enough to spot any stray witches, before they noticed him.

He kept off the crunchy gravel of the drive, and padded silently along the lawn, moving as quickly as he could. Up ahead, he could feel more than hear the presence of many. Magic hummed in the air.

Hunter was surprised that Sophie and her minions hadn't just tried blasting down the front door of the Manor. Instead, they were hovering on the border of the estate, as though they were still wary of the protection the Manor offered its occupants – and still wary of Hunter.

They were near the location of the last battle of Little Hanting. In fact... they were exactly at that location.

Hunter felt uneasy as he moved close enough to see the milling crowd. He tried to count them and estimated two hundred or more.

Suddenly in the centre of the masses, Hunter saw her. Sophie. Her dark brown hair tumbled down her shoulders, her face tanned from the summer sun. Hunter had forgotten how beautiful she was. Obviously motherhood suited her.

Sophie stood with her arms open, her lips moving. Hunter was too far away to hear her chant, but a chill crept up his spine.

Hunter silently swore. He had heard rumours of this ritual, but had never witnessed it. Less than a year ago, more than fifty witches had died violently on this spot. Today Sophie was channelling it.

Having seen enough, Hunter wasted no time and blinked straight back to the Manor.

"Hunter, what news?" Marks asked.

Hunter turned to see Anthony Marks and General Hayworth standing by the window, both armed.

"Not good, sirs." Hunter reported. "At least two hundred individuals, plus the Shadow Witch is tapping into the power left by the last battle."

Marks swore violently enough to make even General Hayworth look surprised.

"We're heavily outnumbered. I doubt we'll be able to call back the troops in time." Hayworth assessed aptly. "We have to retreat."

Hunter blanched at the idea of abandoning his family home, the famous Astley Manor. But there were more important things to protect than a pile of bricks, surely?

Without warning, Hunter's chest constricted, and a voice rang through his head.

"Astley, give yourself to me, or I shall destroy everything in my path to find you. You have two minutes."

"Sophie." Hunter gasped as air flooded his lungs again. He looked up at Hayworth and Marks, and in that moment he could tell that both men had heard the voice too.

96

"Don't you bloody dare." Hayworth growled.

Hunter scowled at them curtailing his sudden urge to be a martyr.

"Right, that's sorted then." Marks announced. "Hayworth, get everyone to the back of the house, have Hunter take them to join Nadira Shah. Hunter, go fetch your mother."

Hunter was about to leave, when Marks grabbed his arm. The older man watched the retreating back of General Hayworth, then turned to Hunter.

"Make sure Hayworth escorts your mother first. He must secure the other side. Then send the others, and go. Promise me you'll go."

"What?" Hunter looked at Marks with a heavy suspicion. "And what do you plan on doing while all this takes place?"

"Stall them." Marks replied. "The Shadow is already building up to end this – you can feel it too, don't deny it."

"But-"

"No time, Hunter. Get everyone out, including yourself – that's an order. Then promise me you'll do everything you can to get a handle on this power of yours. It may prove to be the decisive weapon."

Lost for words, Hunter nodded numbly.

Before any further argument came up, Marks stepped back. He looked on the verge of saying something more, but just shook his head and walked away.

Hunter caught his breath. Now was not the time for emotion! He turned and ran up the main staircase, rounding the corner to his mother's wing of the house.

"Mother!" He yelled as he flung the door open.

"What now, George?" Mrs Astley's voice came from the dining area she'd had Charles set up for her.

97

"We need to go. Now." Hunter replied. "The witches have us surrounded."

Mrs Astley blinked, taking this in. "How very inconvenient, I've just made a pot of tea."

Mrs Astley sat there, looking at her pale blue teapot for a regretful moment. Then with a sigh she got to her feet. "Is there time to pack?"

"No mother." Hunter answered firmly.

"Well, let us go then." Mrs Astley commanded. "If things are so dire, I cannot understand why you are dallying, George!"

Hunter looked at his mother with surprise, but Mrs Astley just huffed and grabbed a coat on the way out. Hunter followed his mother downstairs, the amount of magic in the air was suffocating, his overwhelmed senses made him jumpy. But Mrs Astley led the way calmly.

The dozen people that had remained at Astley Manor were huddled near the library in the recesses of the house. Hunter was relieved to see his team amongst them and took a moment to do a head count.

"Everyone's here, Hunter." Halbrook snapped. "Except Marks."

"He's rear guard." Hunter replied shortly, pushing his way through. He noticed that a section of the wall had been cleared of all pictures and clutter in anticipation of use.

"You're front guard." Hunter added, placing his hand on the wall. "Escort Mrs Astley though, and secure the other side."

General Hayworth looked affronted at being ordered around by the younger man, and there was the gut-wrenching realisation dawning on his face at what Marks was really up to.

But before he could collect his thoughts and argue, a very determined blonde battle-ax linked her arm through his. Despite the fact of the difference in height and build, the petite Mrs Astley led the General to the wall.

Whether it was in compliance through shock, or the sense of duty awakening, Hayworth stepped forward.

Hunter concentrated on opening a link and watched as Hayworth and his mother vanished through the solid wall. With a curt nod, the rest of the men and women filed through, until only his team was left. Sweat was breaking out at the strain of holding it open, but the four remained, in a protective circle around him.

"Go." Hunter ordered.

"Hunter…" James started.

"Go." He repeated. "I'll follow. I promise."

James sighed at his friend's stubbornness but signalled to the others. Without another word, they left.

Hunter dropped his hand from the wall and let the link go. He stood panting for a moment, then turned in the direction of the front hallway. He had spent less than five minutes here. Was he too late to stop Marks? Probably.

Was he too late to save him? Possibly, but he was going to take that chance anyway.

Not wasting a moment, Hunter focused on the location of the witches, then closed his eyes. Hunter felt the familiar pressure close around him, increasing as he attempted to move closer to the source of his distress, until it was suffocating.

Hunter tried to push through again but found a blockade of magic. Even though he wasn't convinced he was physically anywhere, Hunter could feel the burning in his lungs from the prolonged lack of oxygen. He had never felt anything like this and started to panic over his inability to set down. A debilitating pain began sharp spikes in his mind, as he found his struggle for control slipping. And fading.

"Hunter!" The female shriek pierced faintly through his conscious.

Then Hunter felt a wedge of energy knock the last of the breath out of him.

Hunter landed with a heavy thud and coughed, gasping at the cool air that was a relief to his lungs. He opened his eyes and spots danced before them, but he could see, of a sort. It was night, but he could make out the long grass that surrounded him.

The next sense to reawaken was his hearing, he could just hear the hurrying of feet, and several people calling his name.

"Here." He choked, then cleared his voice. He raised his arm sluggishly to make his point. "Here!"

The feet came closer, and Hunter felt a pair of hands run over him in assessment.

"He's ok." James' familiar voice came through. "What happened?"

Hunter sat up, which seemed a good idea at first, but quickly made his head throb again.

"Hunter, where's Marks?" General Hayworth insisted.

Hunter sighed and hung his head. "I tried. I tried to save him." His voice came out as weak as his argument.

There was an abrupt roar, which took Hunter by surprise, as Hayworth turned and swore at the night sky. Anthony Marks had been an ally, and had become a close friend.

Ian moved into Hunter's eye line and pulled a small stone out of his pocket. "A distress signal was sent to Nadira. Hopefully her witch-hunters will be on the lookout." Ian turned the stone in his palm, before re-pocketing it.

Chapter Fifteen

Nadira's patrols found them within a couple of hours and that same night, Hunter and the other survivors were housed in cramped, but welcome accommodation.

It was nearly midday by the time Hunter dragged himself out of bed by the following day. His limbs felt like lead after the previous night, and his head pounded as though he'd downed a bottle of whisky.

As soon as he left his sleeping quarters, he bumped into Alannah, who recognised his need for coffee and steered him to the nearest source. Once he had his second cup, Ian arrived and let Hunter know that he had been requested for a meeting.

Hunter allowed himself to feel relief that his team was alive and well, before he succumbed to the dread of the meeting ahead. He hated meetings; he had often made James go as his representative when the old Council at Oxford expected his presence. But Hunter guessed that he couldn't get out of this one. If anything, he respected Anthony Marks too much to miss it.

The meeting came and went; it was exactly how Hunter imagined it would be. With frayed tempers and 'what ifs'. It didn't matter, a great man was still dead. After they had lost George "Young" Astley and Brian Lloyd; Anthony Marks was one of the last of that generation.

Oh no, wait, there was Gareth Halbrook too. Hunter thought that fate had a cruel sense of humour that he was still alive, when they had lost so many good guys. At least Halbrook was posted down in London with Sergeant Dawkins and was well out of the way.

During the meeting they had quickly discussed Mark's successor, all eyes turning expectantly towards Hunter.

"I nominate Nadira Shah." He had immediately voiced, surprising them all – none more than Nadira herself.

There were no objections to the promotion, and Nadira was named the first female leader of the Malleus Maleficarum Council. The congratulations on such a momentous occasion were diluted by the mourning for a good man.

*****

Hunter took a couple of days to recover from his suspended time in nothingness. Outwardly he was very subdued. Inward, he was scared. It was a wake-up call that he knew next to nothing about his powers. Had he been foolish in using them so frequently when he was unaware of his limits? The threat of the witches' rebellion had made him desperate enough to rush in, head on.

And he'd almost died. Oh, Hunter had come close to death on countless occasions, but it was different when an enemy was going to kill you, rather than his own ignorance.

If it hadn't been for that final push... Hunter thought back to the moment when he'd been catapulted away. He

103

didn't recall doing something, at that point he was close to incapable of planning anything. But he had instances in his past when he'd acted subconsciously. The image of a church brought to rubble flashed into his thoughts.

Yes, it had to be that. Because the only other explanation... that was too hard to take in, and Hunter purposefully refused to think of her.

James drifted in and out while Hunter recovered, much like he had done at the beginning of the year. He was concerned for his friend again, not wanting Hunter to lapse into depression once more.

General Hayworth had drilled Hunter over every detail of what had occurred at the Manor, and Hunter had replied honestly, but perfunctorily. It was only when he repeated it to James one afternoon that Hunter felt the reality of it stab him afresh.

James chewed his lip, worried. "Truth is, we don't know shit about what you can do. With the most extensive library in the UK, we've found nowt substantial for months."

Hunter shifted, trying to get comfortable on the awful camp bed he'd been given. "A library we no longer have." He muttered, feeling a spark of anger, knowing that Sophie and her minions might have destroyed it all by now. Or at the very least, would have pawed through all the contents.

James shrugged, he loved Astley Manor, but that wasn't the point he was trying to make. "We was getting nowhere, mate. Maybe you need another trip to Italy."

Hunter narrowed his eyes, remembering his last holiday to Italy, when he had first met Sophie.

James could tell where his friend's thoughts were going, and he was quick to clarify. "Look, it's the home of the Benandanti. If you're gonna find anything, it'll be there."

Hunter groaned and rested his head back against the wall. "The Benandanti were killed hundreds of years ago, I think that's the definition of a cold trail. Besides, I'm needed here. I am not going to leave you guys facing the witches alone, while I'm off on a wild goose chase."

"But it could answer everything!" James argued. "It'd be worth the risk."

"James, things are only going to get worse here, I can't leave." Hunter replied calmly. "Be honest, if you were in my position, you would do the same."

James sighed and muttered something beneath his breath, then stood up to leave.

"Just... don't leave it too late."

Chapter Sixteen

A few weeks after they had relocated to Manchester, they had company.

Sergeant Dawkins arrived in an old jeep, accompanied by three other soldiers. He was ushered straight into a room with the General and was introduced to Nadira.

"Must have been a long journey. Why did you drive? Hunter could have brought you." The General mused while he put the kettle over a portable stove and dug out the rations of coffee.

Dawkins looked over at Hunter. "No offence, General, but nothing short of a life or death emergency will entice me to travel with Mr Astley again."

Hunter looked up, a little surprised at Dawkins' boldness. "Colin, I'm hurt. You know I'm just looking for another opportunity to make you faint."

The sergeant tried to keep a serious face, but a smile flashed over his lips.

"Ok, down to business." Dawkins pushed on. "We've got a good handle on London. It's too big to know we've covered everything, but it turns out the witch-hunter running things, Tyler, knows what he's doing."

"Tyler who?" Nadira asked.

Dawkins looked a little sheepish. "I've been down there a month, and I still can't pronounce his surname. Begins with an M. But yeah, Tyler – tall, imposing guy, used to part-time as a lawyer..." Dawkins looked about, hoping something would sound familiar. "2nd gen, used to report to the London Bridge branch."

"A 2nd gen?" Hunter echoed, surprised that such an important role would go to such a new family.

"Not every higher generation witch-hunter is made for leadership." Dawkins replied drily, with more than a tad of insinuation. "Tyler has a good network of allies down there. And then there's the wiccans. There's a lot of wiccans."

"London has the densest population of them." Hunter suddenly reeled out. "It's a very... accepting city."

Dawkins looked over at the unnecessary interruption. "Well, they've been very helpful."

The sergeant looked over to his General. "Sir, I know your intel points to an attack on the capital, but we need to be prepared for elsewhere. We are strong there, possibly too strong for the witch army. I can't imagine they'd throw their lives away on uncertain victory with high prices."

Hayworth nodded, as he listened to his sergeant's opinion. "I will take this into consideration, Dawkins. But until we have firm proof, let us proceed as though London will be their target."

Chapter Seventeen

"Hunter!"

The cry rang through the makeshift barracks. It was nearly 10pm, and Hunter was trying to get some sleep before his turn on watch duty in the early hours. It was Hallowe'en, and they were taking their watch duties seriously.

"Hunter!" General Hayworth's familiar voice blasted through the silence.

Hunter cracked open an eye and groaned. "Yes sir."

"Emergency signal from Dawkins. Get your team and get to London. Now."

"What?" Hunter asked, now fully awake. He threw back the bed sheets and grabbed his trousers from the pile of clothes on the floor.

"Dawkins sent an emergency signal through the wiccan stones. I need you to go assess the situation. We'll be mobilizing here if he needs back-up."

Hunter nodded, as he pulled on his shirt and hunted for his stab vest. He was still checking his gun when the door opened again. This time James walked in, followed by Ian,

Maria and Alannah. They were all kitted up and looked ready to go.

"We got the message, let's go." James announced.

Hunter felt a wave of respect at how quickly his team responded, followed by a wavering doubt on his ability to get them from Manchester to London safely. He'd done a few practise runs with James, but that didn't completely eradicate his worries.

But he didn't say a word and waited for his team to take their positions. Hunter counted to three, then closed his eyes and let his focus shift.

There was the familiar, suffocating darkness, followed by the cool air of their destination. Hunter opened his eyes to the sight of the MMC's London Bridge base.

"You took long enough."

Hunter spun round to see Dawkins standing by a black window. He ignored the sergeant's snarky comment. "What's happened?"

Dawkins didn't reply immediately, something outside at ground level was occupying his attention.

"The witches have gathered to burn us alive. You've got to appreciate the irony."

Hunter frowned and moved to join him. They must have been ten floors up, which made the angle incredibly awkward, but Hunter could make out the orange glow at the base of the building.

"We're about to burn to death? Great." Ian stated in his usual dry manner.

"Care to explain, Colin?" James asked.

Dawkins looked over at him. "I was wrong over how secure we were. The new mayor and his team switched sides. They must have been planning it for a while, maybe they never really believed that we could permanently take

London back from the witches. The wiccans split, the majority staying with us, but still a sizeable group joined the witches."

"Casualties?" Hunter asked.

"We're not sure yet, sir." Dawkins reported formally. "Tyler went down in the first attack, along with a dozen others. After I sent the alert, I saw we were outnumbered and ordered a retreat. The rest of our forces have scattered, with orders to meet at the MMC branch in Oxford asap."

"And you stayed behind, Colin?" James frowned at his friend's bravado. He only hoped the sergeant didn't have ideas of martyrdom. They were still reeling from the loss of Anthony Marks.

"I'd already sent the emergency call to you, I had to await your arrival and fill you in. I didn't trust leaving a note to be adequate."

"Um, sorry to break this up guys." Ian interrupted, the tall sergeant standing by the next window. "But I think they've set the building on fire."

The rest of the group pushed closer to the window and it seemed true, the orange glow had grown fiercer, and smoke began to cloud visibility of the stars.

"Do we engage them?" Maria asked, as she checked her gun.

"We'll get revenge for Anthony Marks." Alannah concurred, her green eyes sparking.

"No." Hunter commanded. "We'll leave and reconvene with the others at Oxford."

There was a moment of silence when everyone looked to Hunter, their disappointment evident.

"Y'know, I thought being part of this team would include a little action. Not acting as glorified messengers."

Ian growled, perfectly expressing the thoughts of the group.

Hunter stood, not sure what to say. To be truthful, he wanted nothing more than to lead them down to the witches baying for their blood, and solve a few problems with violence. But someone here had to be logical and sensible. Bloody hell, why did it have to be him.

"Look, we can go down there and repel a few witches before we die. Or let's not be cocky, we might toast in the inferno on the way." Hunter snapped, feeling his own frustration at the prolonged passive nature he'd adopted. "There is no guarantee that the Shadow is with them, and I won't waste your lives despatching a few of her servants. I promise, the time will come when we face her – soon."

Hunter looked from face to determined face, when eventually his team conceded.

There was a cough from the side of the room. "Well, if you're all done team motivating, do you think we could get out of here?" Dawkins asked, hardly able to keep the sarcasm out of his voice.

Hunter shot the sergeant a suitably dirty look, but held out his arms in what was becoming the usual manner. Without a word, his team stepped in and held onto him. Only Dawkins hung back, the nerves finally beginning to show as he looked down at Hunter's outstretched arm.

"Any time, Colin." James snapped, ready to get this over with.

Dawkins swallowed nervously, then gingerly held onto Hunter's forearm.

Hunter didn't give him the chance to change his mind, and immediately blinked from the burning building at London Bridge, to the grounds of the old MMC headquarters in Oxford.

As he felt the cold, fresh breeze on his face, and the light spattering of rain, Hunter looked about him. This had been his MMC office, where he had been registered when young, and where he had made constant trips for reports and meetings since he had become a fully-fledged witch-hunter six years ago.

It was as familiar and frustrating a building as any workplace.

Or it had been.

Hunter looked at it now and saw only rubble. A couple of walls still stood, useless monuments to what had once been. Oxford was the oldest MMC headquarters, and as such was the historical seat of the Council, as well as storing most processed amulets from the binding process.

The Shadow Witch had hit this place first, after she had procured the Key from Hunter's dear friend, Charlotte King. The Key had released all the bound power the MMC had been storing away for generations – not a good system, in hindsight.

It was painful for Hunter to look on to his old, ruined offices. A reminder that, despite the wheels set irreversibly in motion in Venice, here the war really started.

A heavy pat on the shoulder brought him back to the present, and Hunter turned to see James looking back at him with a similar pain in his usually light brown eyes.

"It's really quiet. Where is everyone?" Alannah asked, looking around uneasily.

"We blinked…" Dawkins gasped out, trying not to retch. "They'll arrive… in a few… hours."

Ian smirked at the sight of General Hayworth's right-hand man so disabled. "Maria and I will make a perimeter check. We'll be back in half an hour." Ian stated, volunteering for the walk. Well, it was better than huddling in the rubble of some building while they waited.

The survivors came slowly, in dribs and drabs. Many had emergency vehicles and used precious fuel to escape the city, and they brought as many as they could with them.

Ian and Maria had found a disused theatre that might be big enough to house them for the night. With the help of James and Alannah, and the locals who awoke to all the noise, food and spare blankets were acquired; and a section of the theatre was cordoned off for first aid.

Hunter had managed to round up Oxford's promising medical students. Despite the witch revolution, they were all here to learn, and still socialised in the same places they had when Hunter had gone to university here. The young meds had come willingly to the theatre, that was now full of people; soldiers, witch-hunters, and helpful locals.

Once the first mad rush of caring for the wounded, and organising the able-bodied had passed, Hunter stepped back to observe the place. Despite the injured, it was warming to see how his old town of Oxford rallied to help them. That was something the witches would never understand, would never overcome in their drive to control all – the average person could step up and do things they would never account for.

*****

Hunter tried to get a few hours' sleep, then the next day he worked alongside Sergeant Dawkins to organise the troops. They would send those willing back to London, to be their eyes and ears, to make sure the people they left behind were not treated too harshly.

113

To the rest, they offered a chance to leave, to go home to safety. Or to go on with them to Manchester, to face the next fight with the witches. Hunter was heartened that nearly every man and woman immediately signed up to travel North.

Leaving Dawkins with the wiccan stones in case of emergency, Hunter took his team back to Manchester that very afternoon, to report to the General all that had occurred.

Chapter Eighteen

The notion that Manchester was the next target of the witches became a firm fact. For the past couple of weeks, ever since London had been hit on Hallowe'en, their wiccan spies had been running back with information. It was the first time all details pointed in one direction.

But this time, they were ready for them.

Nadira and General Hayworth had divided their forces into groups, bolstered by the volunteers from the city. Hunter looked over his group, noting how soldiers now outnumbered witch-hunters, after they had been targeted so fiercely by the witches. Both were outnumbered by the citizens of Manchester and the surrounding area – it was cheering to see so many step up to defend their city, their home.

Hunter was glad to see the familiar faces of his team in the sea of strangers. They sat together, outwardly looking calm and ready, a highly skilled team that was comforting to the rest that were new to battle. But Hunter knew them well enough now to see the nervous tells. James was twisting the gold ring on his right hand that blocked minor spells; Alannah sat polishing an already gleaming knife;

Maria fiddled with the zips on her stab vest and jacket; and Ian – well, Hunter had yet to work out what nervous tick that man had, he was constantly calm and in control.

Hunter drifted back to his friends, causing them to look up.

"You sure about…" Alannah started. She coughed and lowered her voice. "You sure about your plan?"

"Course he is." James interrupted, then glanced at Hunter. "Aren't you?"

"Already told you James, if you don't feel confident, you can stay here and keep charge of the others." Hunter replied, repeating an earlier suggestion. "The four of us can handle it."

James snorted. "Yeah right, as if I've ever hesitated in following you into madness."

Hunter just smiled in response, not sure James should be describing his leadership skills and plans as 'madness'. At least, not in public.

Hunter was saved from trying to come up with a suitably intelligent reply by the sudden headache that accompanied magic and spells being cast. It was immense, almost over-whelming, and Hunter took a moment to tune it out enough to concentrate. He could see Alannah making the same mental struggle, as the other three just looked on expectantly.

"They're here." Hunter murmured. The witches had come. They were about a mile to the south, if his senses were correct.

Hunter was distracted by a sharp pain in his side. He pulled the wiccan stone out of his pocket, watching as the lump of quartz flashed hot, then faded back to its normal smoky colour. He held it up for the others to see, as proof that their allies were engaging.

"It's time."

Hunter turned to the masses and shouted for attention. The chatter and general noise immediately died down, and everyone looked to him.

He took a deep breath, realising they were expecting some sort of glorious, heroic speech – because wasn't that what he was to these people, a hero they had heard could do miracles and lead them to victory?

But Hunter's throat closed up at the very thought.

"Let's move out." He shouted in a strangled voice.

There was a snicker besides him.

"Oh aye, very inspiring, Hunter." James didn't even try to hide his amusement as he watched his friend struggle over something so simple. "I hope that speech doesn't go down in history – really shite final words."

Hunter was tempted to retaliate, but he remembered his audience. They probably wouldn't like to see the man they were trusting with their lives, beating a friend.

So, Hunter turned and nodded to the rest of his team.

The hundred or so men and women picked up their arms and followed Hunter to the south, where magic was bristling so strongly, Hunter was surprised the 1st gens couldn't feel it.

There was a blast of light to one side as they approached, followed by the screams of the spell's victims. The ground shook with the strength of magic that ran across it, and the wind picked up, whipping through the forms and fields that had become the site of battle.

As they approached within sight of the witches, Hunter saw the illusions of monsters that were hastily thrown up to gain the witches time to bring out harder spells. Fire burst out on their left flank, as salamanders and fire-wrought creatures moved into existence.

117

Hunter threw up his shield, the illusions of monsters faded to nothing. The fire wavered, but having enough dry fuel to sustain it, it spread on.

The witches hesitated, seeing their spells falter, and knowing that the infamous Hunter Astley must be behind it. Hunter took advantage of the moment and led his fighters on, forcing the witches in close combat that served knives and guns better than magic.

Hunter cut a swathe through his opponents. His anger spurred him on, with each thrust of his knife, broken neck, or shot to the heart, he was avenging Anthony Marks, and countless other witch-hunters and innocents that had been caught in this rebellion. He did not spare a thought for the blood that coated his hands and arms, he ignored the cuts and wounds he gained as adrenaline surged through his body. But he was aware that he had pushed further than anyone else, and started to back up, enemies on all sides able to pick him out.

There was a gunshot, close enough that Hunter could hear it over the fray, and one of the witches before him crumpled to the ground.

A pat on his shoulder made Hunter start, but he turned to see James and Maria moving up to join him, Maria turning her gun to her next victim.

There was a wave of magic so strong, Hunter was nearly knocked over. By the time he regained his balance, he recognised the swirling clouds overhead, and felt the now-familiar rhythm of Sophie's magic. The wind picked up, and Hunter swore.

"Maria!" James' voice cut through the noise.

Hunter turned to see Maria unmoving on the ground, and James dispatching the witch that had managed to take down their best gunman.

Hunter felt a renewed strike of magic against his shield, but he pushed it back with a mental shove, then knelt by Maria.

James was already searching for signs of life with shaking hands. He then gave a sigh, his shoulders drooping. "She's got a pulse."

James closed his eyes and muttered something to himself. If Hunter didn't know him better, he would have sworn it was a prayer of thanks.

Hunter was distracted by something sharp cutting into the back of his exposed neck. He looked up to see wind-driven ice starting weakly but gaining momentum. Cries of pain went up around him as his allies were forced to stagger back. The witches seemed immune from the sharp fragments, or at least were not the intended victims.

"Hunter, we need to move." Ian barked as he ran up, Alannah on his heels.

"Maria?" Alannah's green eyes were filled with fresh worry above a blood-stained cheek.

"She's alive, she'll be fine." Hunter replied quickly, determined to keep positive.

James huddled over Maria, protecting her from the cutting ice. "Hunter, I can't... I need to..."

Hunter put a hand on his friend's shoulder. "I understand. Get her to safety. We'll go ahead."

James nodded and swallowed hard. He scooped up Maria, who stayed lifeless in his arms. "Good luck." He said to the others, then began to jog in the direction of their back line.

Chapter Nineteen

Hunter stayed just long enough to watch James get to a safe distance. He was surprised to feel let down; this had been the first time that James had chosen not to be at his side to face life-threatening danger. Hunter grimaced at his own thoughts – James was not a coward, far from it. But personally insisting that he take care of Maria... he must care for her more than Hunter had guessed.

"So, what now?" Alannah asked.

Hunter glanced from Alannah to Ian, they both awaited his next orders.

"We carry on as planned." He answered with a shrug.

There was a flicker of fear from Alannah, but Ian just nodded.

"Right, let's go." The sergeant simply said, then started in the opposite direction James had taken – further into danger, instead of away from it.

Hunter hurried after him, then moved into the lead. Despite the fact that Hunter's senses were nearly over-whelmed by the volume of magic and casting witches, Sophie's magic rang out as a clear chord of power. With an unsettling ease, Hunter followed it towards the source.

He didn't trust himself to blink them safely to her location, so they had to take the mundane route. As they fought their way through loose groups of witches, they came more heavily under attack. Hunter doubled the shield around the three of them, reluctantly letting his shield fade from the other fighters. He couldn't possibly maintain both.

In a thick bubble of anti-magic, the trio pushed forward. Hunter was glad to have his two best fighters with his, as Ian floored a witch, and Alannah made sure he didn't get up again.

Hunter could feel Sophie's presence getting closer, and finally spotted her. Her witches had pulled back, as though even they could not stand to get close to her magic. Her long brown hair was half-falling out of a plait and she was dressed for combat, with the stab vest that Hunter had given her on top of a short, dark jacket and jeans.

Everything was muted, and everyone seemed to clear the space between Hunter and the Shadow Witch. A hundred yards apart, Hunter's pulse raced with anticipation – it would all be over now.

Sophie stopped mid-spell and faced the witch-hunter. Without her support, the clouds and the wind settled, and the ice eased off.

Taking a deep breath, Hunter started to move cautiously forward, Ian and Alannah flanking him. He was aware of the eyes that turned their way.

Hunter felt Sophie's magic curling and preparing for release. Within a heartbeat, his own power reacted with it. A visible dome of energy crackled over them, and Hunter could only stare at it in wonder. Was this him?

"Astley!" Sophie snarled. "Don't do this."

Ah, she was pissed off, so it had to be his doing.

"I can't stop it. Even if I wanted to, I would not." Hunter replied. "Your witches are on their own, now."

Her witches were powerful, but without the aid of their Shadow, Hunter hoped they could be overcome.

Sophie's lip curled as she wildly looked around her for a point of weakness. Finding none, she suddenly became calm. She took a few steps forward, her movements achingly familiar.

"So... what's the plan now, Hunter? Kill the big bad witch while she's defenceless?" Sophie asked with a sigh, knowing how her lover saw her now.

"It has to happen, Sophie." Hunter replied. "It's the only way to stop them."

Sophie gave a bitter laugh. "Oh, that you believe that! I miss your optimism, Hunter. So... will you kill me?"

Hunter fought to keep his expression neutral. "Me, or others."

There was a flash of metal, as one of Alannah's throwing knives whipped across the distance. Ian pulled out his gun and fired off half a dozen rounds.

Sophie raised both hands, and the bullets slowed and stopped in an invisible barrier. She looked surprised at the block, but her expression turned to pain, as the knife sank into her upper chest. Alannah, by mistake or design, hitting the weak point of her armour, near the neck.

Hunter steeled himself, as Sophie's scream rent the air, and she dropped to her knees.

Sophie flicked her long brown hair out of the way, as it sought to escape, and her furious eyes focused on Alannah. "You little bitch!"

Sophie took a deep breath and grabbed the knife, wrenching it out with another scream. She gasped, and wiped a hand over the wound, where the blood flow was already ceasing and healing.

"Do you really think you can kill me?" Sophie spat, then turned the knife in her hand and threw it with all her strength at the shell-shocked Alannah.

Alannah's eyes widened as she witnessed her own knife being used against her. There was the sudden movement of a huge bulk, who stepped in the way, and grunted as the knife embedded itself in his back.

Ian gripped Alannah tightly by the arms, and gave a reassuring smile, before he slumped.

Hunter's breathing increased, his pulse speeding. His window of opportunity was closing up and everything was going wrong.

Sophie smiled, and waved a blood-stained hand. "Bye."

Without thinking, Hunter charged towards her. Already her image was fading to the grey of shadows, but Hunter reached out desperately. He felt that familiar soft, warm nothingness, followed by the cold wind and hard ground beneath his feet.

Gasping, Hunter got his bearings. There was light and noise, and deafening magic a mile or so to his right. And directly in front of him was Sophie.

"You shouldn't have come." She said softly, pity in her usually cold eyes.

Hunter shrugged. "You didn't give me much choice."

He slowly removed a long knife from his belt and watched as Sophie silently did the same. With an unspoken signal, they started to circle, each watching for weak spots in the other. Then they attacked.

Hunter was surprised at Sophie's speed, but didn't have time to marvel, as he followed up his attack with deflections and taking a step back that only intensified Sophie's attack.

But Hunter wasn't the best in the MMC for nothing, and caught a lapse in her guard and forced her to retreat in turn.

They both backed off to catch their breath, and Sophie took a moment to wipe blood from a new cut on her arm.

"You've remembered all your training." Hunter remarked.

Sophie bit back a smile. "I had a good teacher."

They came to again, the strike and parry patterns getting longer and more intricate.

"You were holding back on me before." Hunter gasped.

"So were you." Sophie countered, her hazel eyes flashing.

Sophie fainted to the left, then tackled him from the right, so that they both lost balance and fell to the floor.

Hunter felt the breath knocked out of him, and suddenly found himself on his back, Sophie straddling his legs to pin them down.

"Well now." She murmured, looking down at Hunter, her gaze warming. "Join me, please Hunter. Together we can set this world straight."

"After you destroyed it?" Hunter snapped back, bringing up his knife in a half-hearted effort.

Sophie easily caught his wrist, and pressed it to his chest. "No, after I destroyed the only reality you knew. Don't mistake comfort and familiarity for something right. Please Hunter, don't you want to be in a world free from all the wrongs you knew were in your Council? Don't you want a world where you could be with me? With your son?"

Hunter stilled at the mention of his son. Where was he now? At home with his grandmother, while his mother went on her killing spree?

"Not at this price." Hunter replied quietly.

Hunter gathered himself, and threw Sophie from him, he scrambled to his feet and glared at her. Hunter pulled out his gun and pointed it at Sophie's chest for a moment, before reluctantly letting it drop.

"You saved me at Astley Manor, didn't you?" Hunter asked. When Sophie made no effort to reply, he sighed. "Consider this a life for a life. Get out of here, Sophie. Take Adam and get away from this fight. If our paths cross again, I will kill you."

Sophie stood, the colour draining from her face. She took a moment to weigh her options, then turned away from Hunter. The shadows thickened about her, and tendril-like wrapped around her form and claimed her. Then she was gone.

Hunter let loose a shaky breath. He really hoped he'd done the right thing. With a quick glance at his surroundings, he blinked back to his friends.

Chapter Twenty

"Are you sure I can't get you anything else?" Alannah crooned, leaning over the hospital bed.

Ian grinned, it was only natural that she'd want to make it up to him – he had taken a knife in the back for her, after all. "No, I'm fine Alannah. Now settle down – I'm getting tired just watching you."

"I can bring you a book, or a change of clothes from camp." Alannah persisted.

"I'm not much of a reader." Ian sighed, relenting a little. "Clothes would be good though. These are a bit…"

"Blood-stained?" Hunter offered, as he leant back in an uncomfortable plastic chair he'd dragged over.

"Tatty." Ian corrected.

It was nearly midday, and it was hard to believe that the battle had only been over for ten hours or so. They had had an obvious victory, decimating the witch army, and driving back the survivors. The mood was incredibly up-beat, the winter suddenly holding the promise of a hard-won peace, there was no way the witches could mount a retaliation any time soon. Now there was only the slow recovery of their own forces to concern themselves with.

Ian was recovering well. He was already bored of staying in his hospital bed, and wasn't about to let a knife wound turn him into an invalid.

Further down the ward, James leant over the bed where Maria lay. The lieutenant had awoken a few hours before, still feeling weak from whatever had hit her. Of course, James had never left her bedside.

Hunter glanced towards them every now and then, but stayed with Ian to give them a bit of privacy. It occurred to him that even the invulnerable Sergeant Ian Grimshaw might need the comfort of a loved one.

"I could bring your partner, if you want company." Hunter offered.

Ian thought about it for a moment, then grinned. "Nah, not just yet. It'd scare him to see me in this state. Wait until I'm looking a little less..."

"Tatty?" Hunter ventured.

Ian chuckled, then winced in pain. He glanced over at James and Maria for the umpteenth time.

"So... how long has that been going on?"

Hunter shrugged. "Four months." He guessed.

"Six." Alannah corrected.

The two guys looked at her, making her blush.

"What?" She challenged. "We may be in the middle of a war with witches, but me and Maria are still allowed girl talk."

"Girl talk?" Hunter echoed. "Why does that phrase fill me with fear?"

Ian chuckled. "I think you're referring to the ability of women to intimately discuss everything and everyone. I'm exempt, right? Too old for that nonsense."

Alannah just grinned in response and winked. "Forty is not old. Well, I think they're good together."

Ian coughed. "They're coming over."

Hunter looked up to see James pushing a wheelchair, with a tired-looking Maria in it.

James glanced around the guilty faces. "What?" He demanded.

"Nothing." Alannah squeaked.

Hunter shrugged. "We were just talking about you, that's all. Maria, how are you feeling?"

"Like I've been hit by a bus." Maria croaked. "S'fine. I don't need the chair, but Mr Protective here..."

"The doctors said rest." James interrupted. "You shouldn't really be out of bed."

"I wanted to hear what happened firsthand." Maria replied with a sigh, then turned expectantly to Hunter.

Hunter looked at the waiting faces of his team, then began to recount what happened last night, starting with Alannah and Ian's part in it. He finished with a less than faithful account, leaving out the fact that he had let Sophie go, making it sound more like she had escaped.

When he finished, there was silence.

"Guns didn't work, knives didn't work, our miracle 7th gen didn't work." Alannah huffed. "I'd like to know what can kill her."

"She's just another witch." James offered, unconvincingly. "She got lucky this time, that's all. Right, Hunter?"

Hunter looked up at the sound of his name but didn't reply. She'd gotten very lucky. But what if they met again, could Hunter kill her?

"What's she like?" Maria croaked. "The Shadow Witch?"

"Suitably scary." Ian answered.

"Beautiful. No one mentioned she was beautiful." Alannah added, gazing at the boys accusingly. "Well Hunter, I can see why you'd not be interested in… anyone, after her."

"Beautiful, huh?" Maria repeated, twisting to look up at James.

"I never noticed." James added, flashing a warning look at Hunter. "She wasn't my type."

Hunter turned to Alannah again. "We've just fought our biggest battle to date, and you want to go over my dating history?"

Alannah grinned, pleased that he'd caught up. "Yup."

Hunter chuckled. "Uh-huh. Well I wasn't interested in her because she was beautiful."

The silence was immediate, and the look of disbelief was shared by all.

"Ok, it might have had a little to do with it." Hunter conceded. "But it wasn't everything."

"Oh aye, there was her sparkling personality." James added, rolling his eyes. "Frigid bitch was the term we used most often, weren't it?"

As the rest of the team laughed, Hunter crossed his arms.

"If you lot are going to take the piss, I'm going."

"Getting back to the main point." Ian said sombrely, as he re-adjusted the pillow behind him. "I refuse to believe that she's impossible to take down."

"You said there were other Shadows." Maria asked, her voice rough. "How did they die?"

"There were two." James confirmed. "One was a thousand years ago. The second was in the forties – the one that Hunter's grandfather killed."

"And how did he do that?" Alannah asked, her big eyes turning to Hunter.

"No one knows. Old George never made an official report of it."

"Did you never ask him?" Ian asked.

"He died when I was very young." Hunter replied quietly. People in his profession didn't have the longest lifespans. The fact that his grandfather had survived into his sixties was impressive. "I don't remember much about him, only that he was a very private and miserable old man. From my father's stories of Old George, that impression was only intensified."

"So, he never shared?" Alannah sounded very disappointed.

"No." James answered. "And we've exhausted every line of research into that area."

"Well, we'll find something." Alannah said, getting to her feet and stretching. "I'm off to get some sleep."

She leant over the bedside and kissed Ian's cheek, then kissed Maria. "I'm glad you two are ok."

Hunter pushed himself out of the uncomfortable chair. "I'll walk you back to your quarters."

He pulled on his coat and scarf, ready to brave the winter weather.

Chapter Twenty-one

Christmas was a suitably joyful time. Despite the fact that the world had not recovered, people were making the most of it and gathered with friends and family. Hard-earned meals were cooked, presents had been rustled together, everything was feeling festive.

It was only five in the afternoon, but already it was dark, as Hunter wandered the streets of Manchester, his hands shoved deep into his pockets, and his shoulders hunched against the cold rain. He saw the firelight, bright in the windows of each home, people casting shadows against the curtains. They were all safe and warm, there had been no witch attack since the post-Hallowe'en battle. Hunter felt a little pride at that. But mostly he felt lonely.

Alannah had gone to her parents; Ian had gone to stay with his partner's family; and James had taken Maria, to introduce her to his aunt and uncle.

James had of course invited Hunter to his family's Christmas, like he did every year. But this year Hunter felt like he would be imposing.

Hunter sighed, his breath fogging before him on this wonderfully miserable, grey Christmas. He reluctantly turned on his heel and headed back towards the MMC camp.

It was quiet. Most of the witch-hunters and soldiers had gone home for the festive occasion, just like Hunter's team. But there were a few that were still milling around like lost souls.

Hunter drifted about until he found who he was looking for – he admitted that only severe loneliness would force him to look for her.

"George, you missed the first course." His mother snapped.

Her beady grey eyes followed the tray of sliced turkey that the ever-faithful Charles was carrying. "I hope this is not more of that regurgitated swill – the processed food."

Hunter made an apologetic face in the direction of the people that had joined his mother's table.

"It is fresh, mother. Charles and I went to the Whitaker farm yesterday to pick up our order." Hunter explained, watching as Charles placed the turkey down and came back with equally farm-fresh, steaming vegetables.

"Hm, very well." Mrs Astley conceded. "Although you know I prefer goose."

Hunter sighed and helped Charles bring in the rest of the food, before he could say anything he could regret. Then he sat down and began what truly resembled a Christmas dinner. Roughly a dozen people sat around the table with them, and after a few awkward introductions and clumsy passes of the sprouts, everyone was cheery and content.

"Room for one more?"

Hunter looked up to see Gareth Halbrook, of all people, hovering at the end of the table. Hunter nearly choked on his potatoes.

"Not for you, no." He said, the words leaving his lips before he could stop them.

"George, cover your mouth." Mrs Astley ordered. "And don't be rude to Mr…?"

She gazed up questioningly with her cool, grey eyes.

"Halbrook. Gareth Halbrook." He answered.

"Halbrook…" Mrs Astley pursed her lips. "Any relation to Derrick Halbrook, from the London Tennis Club?"

Halbrook paused, not expecting that. "No."

Mrs Astley exhaled and relaxed her shoulders a little. "Oh, then I suppose you are the Halbrook that has been a thorn in the side of both my son, and my late husband."

Hunter bit his cheek to stop himself from laughing, as Halbrook looked well and truly on the back foot.

"Now look 'ere, just 'cos I don't worship the famous Astley family, don't mean-"

"You truly have the most atrocious way of speaking." Mrs Astley interrupted, her eyes narrowing in Halbrook's direction, before flicking to Hunter. "I thought your friend James was bad, he's positively eloquent next to this, this…"

"Hey, now!" Halbrook cut in. "I didn't ask for your opinion. I thought I was being proper polite asking to join you lot – it's not as though we're at Astley Manor where you're queen of bloody court."

Mrs Astley considered him for a moment longer. "Hm, I like him. Sit down and help yourself, Mr Halbrook. Shall I ask Charles to send for a bib, or are you quite educated with a fork?"

Halbrook looked dazed and a little speechless, but gathering that the result of this interaction was that he was allowed to sit and eat, he parked himself in a spare chair.

He leant across to grab an empty plate from the stack and muttered to Hunter. "Why don't you send her off against the witches? We'd have won by New Year."

Mrs Astley accepted another glass of wine from the very nervous-looking young woman sat next to her.

"Speaking of the New Year, George, I intend to go home. You can do your little magic trick and take me."

"Mother." Hunter started carefully. "The Manor is deemed unsafe. I cannot let you go there."

Mrs Astley looked at her son, her sharp grey eyes not understanding. "While I respect your concern for my safety, it is not for you to allow me anything. Astley Manor must have an Astley in it, it is not up for discussion. Besides, Mrs Harsmith wrote to me lately, to inform me that more of the villagers have returned to Little Hanting. She tells me that no witch nor human has been near the Manor for a month."

"Mother-"

Mrs Astley held up a hand to silence him. "That is quite enough of that, George. I have made up my mind. Now go, help Charles bring in the next course."

Hunter cursed beneath his breath, getting to his feet to help the long-suffering Charles.

Halbrook smirked at the mother and son interaction, but was quick to hide it before the formidable Mrs Astley noticed.

Chapter Twenty-two

The next few months passed by in a haze of peace. A year since the witch rebellion ruined so many lives, people were beginning to make the most of their new world. The communities were well on their way to rebuilding what was destroyed, and despite the lack of technology and slow communication, the people fell into a new routine. A new normal.

Which included maintaining the great British tradition of going to the pub. On evenings when his whole team were free from duty, Hunter and the others frequented a nice place that was quite close to the MMC base.

The building was old-fashioned, with stone walls, and dark timbers that were well-suited to the atmosphere created by lamps and candles. It was quite a large establishment, but still managed to always feel cosy. It was popular with the locals and the witch-hunters alike, with good ale. Occasionally it was extra-popular, when a band would come in to play live, and the tables would be pushed to the sides to make room for a dance floor.

Hunter enjoyed the live music; it always made an evening that little bit more special. The band that was on tonight was good, although it made Hunter smile to watch the singer trying to fight to be heard without a microphone.

"What are you smirking at?" Alannah shouted over the noise.

Hunter shook his head, not about to explain himself. Instead he offered to get in another round. He made his way to the bar and looked over his shoulder. Alannah and Ian sat on the table he'd recently vacated. James and Maria were on the dance floor – Hunter grimaced at James' lack of co-ordination. Poor Maria.

He quickly got served and carried the three pints and a bottle of white wine on a tray back to their table.

"You know, on a night like this, I can almost forget that the war is happening." Alannah's sentiment lost a little by her need to shout over the music.

Hunter passed her the bottle of wine. "Make sure Maria gets at least some of that."

Alannah grinned. "I don't think she'd notice."

Her green eyes turned in the direction of the dance floor, where despite the upbeat song, Maria and James danced in each other's arms, circling slowly amidst the more energetic dancers. Hunter watched them for a minute, they always acted so professionally around the others, this sort of down-time was the only time he ever witnessed them act as a couple.

Hunter looked away, surprised to feel a little jealous that his best friend was so happy. He picked up his pint and engaged Ian in a conversation about the vehicles the MMC had managed to collect; which moved on to the different techniques of hot-wiring, in which Ian was almost as proficient as James.

Alannah sat quietly at the table, a third-wheel to the conversation. When she finished her wine, she set the glass

136

purposefully down on the table. "I'm bored. You guys want to dance?"

Both Hunter and Ian looked at her, their matching expressions telling how very little they wanted to dance. Ian was the first to crack, seeing how determined Alannah was. The sergeant stood up and took one of her hands.

"Come on, Hunter. If I'm dancing, you are too." Ian ordered.

Hunter sighed, but dutifully pushed himself to his feet. He took Alannah's other hand, the little Welsh girl almost bouncing over the fact that she'd bullied them both.

The band had just moved into another fast track, the song a popular one with the crowd, who filed to the floor. Luckily, Hunter could get away with the minimum amount of movement from side to side. He kept his eyes fixed towards the stage, rather than allow himself to notice that people were watching him in his embarrassment.

James and Maria had broken from their close contact dance, and came to join the rest of them. Maria was shaking her hips next to Alannah, and James was... well, James was jumping around and making a fool out of himself. Hunter saw that even Ian was chuckling at him.

They stayed together for another song, then Ian put his hands up in defeat, and left the youngsters on the dance floor, in favour of his beer.

The band played the final chord of one song and moved seamlessly into the next. The tempo had suddenly slowed. Hunter noticed the active dancing being replaced by couples gently dancing together, including James and Maria, who drifted away from him.

Alannah stood awkwardly beside Hunter, and when he looked in her direction, she gave a hopeful little shrug.

Sighing, and feeling that he might regret this, Hunter slipped his right arm about Alannah's slim waist, and took her right hand in his left, holding it close to his chest. He led in an informal pattern, Alannah was stiff at first, but soon relaxed, and softened to lean against him, her cheek against his chest.

"I thought you couldn't dance." Alannah remarked.

"I can dance, I just choose not to." Hunter corrected.

He twirled her out elegantly, then pulled her back a little less so. They both laughed as they collided.

"I need a drink." Hunter admitted. "Dancing is dangerous."

He dropped his contact with Alannah and without waiting for her, made his way back to the table. Ian gave him an odd look as he re-joined him but didn't say anything.

Alannah pushed her hair away from her sweaty forehead, as she looked down at the table with greatly reduced drinks. "My round?" She said breathlessly, then turned and practically skipped in the direction of the bar.

With Alannah gone, Ian leant forward. "I hope you know what you're doing."

Hunter sat in confusion at his statement, but before he had chance to answer, they gained extra company at their table.

"Hey, do you mind if we sit here? Everywhere else is full."

Hunter looked up, to see who the voice belonged to. The first thing he noticed was the legs in skin-tight jeans, and the long black hair, followed by the pretty face.

"Sure." He said, waving to the spare seats. "I'm Hunter, this is Ian."

138

The black-haired girl flashed him a smile and sat next to him. "I'm Kayleigh, this is Tegan." She responded, motioning to her blonde friend that sat shyly on the other side of her.

"Nice to meet you both."

"You don't sound like you're from round here, Hunter." Kayleigh remarked.

"Guilty, I'm from a village near Oxford." Hunter answered, leaning closer to be heard over the music.

"Really, what brings you to Manc, then?"

Hunter grinned; how many times had he gotten into conversation with a normal person, and had to come up with some fake job that dictated where he went. He could never tell the truth, because no one had known about his organisation. Now, though... "I'm with the witch-hunters."

Across the table, Ian gave him a disappointed look. Disappointed, but as he glanced at Kayleigh, unsurprised.

The black-haired girl grinned. "You're kidding me! Really?"

"Not interrupting, am I?" Alannah called out, as she slid a tray of drinks onto the table, her green eyes narrowing in the direction of the newcomers.

"No, hi! Girls, this is Alannah, she's a witch-hunter too. And Alannah, this is..." Hunter broke off, struggling to remember their names.

"Kayleigh and Tegan." Kayleigh repeated, looking amused, rather than offended at his memory loss.

"Nice to meet you." Alannah said stonily. "You know, I think I might head home, I didn't realise how late it was."

Hunter looked up, realising that she did look a little pale. Probably too much wine and dancing.

Noticing that Hunter wasn't playing the part Alannah had hoped, Ian stood up. "I'll walk you home."

Alannah snatched up her coat and left without another word.

"What was that about?" Kayleigh asked.

"Dunno." Hunter muttered.

*****

The following morning Jonathan moved through the witch-hunter's compound towards the sleeping quarters but stopped when he saw Hunter.

"Hey, I was just coming to find you. Were you on duty?" Jonathan asked, frowning. He wasn't sure Hunter's attire was suitable for night duty.

"What? No, it was my evening off." Hunter replied distractedly.

Jonathan paused, then filled in the blanks. His confusion changed to amusement. "You've only just got back in? You'll get a reputation."

"Already got one." Hunter huffed, as he shoved his cold hands into his pockets. "Was there something you wanted? Other than discussing my promiscuity."

"Promiscuity? Is that your snobbish way of admitting you're a manwhore?"

Hunter narrowed his eyes in the direction of the wiccan. "Have you been talking to James?"

Jonathan finally broke into a grin. "That obvious, huh? On top of other things discussed, James wanted me to chat with you – about magic."

Hunter cringed at the very thought. He might be a little more open-minded than the old him that saw witches and magic in black and white, and sneered at wiccans as a pesky shade of grey – but he wasn't ready to fully embrace magic.

140

"Fine." He relented. "But let's go inside, it's freezing."

"You're just nesh." Jonathan chuckled at the soft southerner, but obediently followed Hunter indoors.

It didn't take long for the two men to acquire vital coffee and headed for an unused office.

"Ok, what did you have to say?" Hunter asked as they sat down.

Jonathan wrapped his hands about his steaming mug, looking up at the witch-hunter. "James came to me for advice. He filled me in on the whole Benandanti thing, including the fact that your research has dried up. As you're not willing to seek them out in Italy-"

"I did not say *never*." Hunter stressed. "It's just a very inappropriate time to leave."

Jonathan held his hands up defensively, and pressed on. "So... short of finding an amiable witch to chat magic with, James and I thought that I might prove helpful."

Hunter frowned, he had not thought of asking magic-users about his own skills, mainly because he was too proud to share his private problems. Which he was equally unlikely to admit.

"Technically it's not magic." Hunter argued.

"No, it's the opposite." Jonathan agreed. "But from what I've heard, and what I've seen for myself, it acts a lot like it."

A sleep-deprived Hunter failed to come up with any logical counter of this point, so instead he leant back in his chair and crossed his arms.

Jonathan tried to hide his smile as he noted the small win. "So first, what can you do?" He asked, blowing on his hot coffee.

Hunter sighed. "Not much. I can travel in a blink, taking others with me. There's a shield I can project, temporarily blocking magic, and bullets on the rare occasion. Oh, and I destroyed a church, once."

"You destroyed a church…" Jonathan echoed, not sure whether to be amused or appalled.

"Mmm, it was quite the scene." Hunter confirmed, thinking back to the night Charlotte had died. "Although I did not know it was my doing until later."

Jonathan took in the mental image, but then shook his head. "Ok, let's focus on the shield. How do you do it?"

Hunter paused, he had never really taken time to dissect and explain it. "I honestly don't know. It seems to happen almost reflexively when spells are being cast. But once it's up, I can move it, expand or contract it…"

Jonathan nodded, looking very serious. "What does it *feel* like?"

"Like… a weight, barely noticeable at first, but tiring the longer I hold it. It's like an extension of me, I can feel everything that hits it." Hunter answered. It felt weird discussing his skills so logically with someone that wasn't James.

"And have you tried to do anything else with your magic?"

"A few things, nothing successful." Hunter replied; the warmth of a blush tickled his neck as he thought back on his foolish attempts. "Lighting candles and light bulbs, picking locks, healing grazes… from what I've read, these are the simplest spells even weak witches can manage."

"From what you've told me, what you possess is not magic, you cannot expect to do the same things." Jonathan reasoned. "Can I suggest something, Hunter? Allow me to train you in the basics of wiccan practices."

142

Hunter scowled, but Jonathan pressed on. "No, listen to me, I may be able to help you. A wiccan's manipulation of magic might have similarities to how you use your anti-magic – we might unlock something new. It can't hurt, can it?"

Although he was far from happy at the prospect, Hunter had to admit that Jonathan's reasoning was sound. Shit. Which meant he had no valid excuse.

"Fine. We'll give it a go."

Chapter Twenty-three

The Malleus Maleficarum Council in Manchester had become the biggest gathering of witch-hunters in the North. New protocols and duties were devised as they went. For the most part, daily life went on in an almost mundane routine; but that was not to say that everything went smoothly. There were still constant threats from smaller covens that tried to stake their ground too near the towns and cities. The MMC were regularly called upon to deal with such threats. It was almost like the old days.

One day in the middle of May, a similar message was brought through to the Council that almost had James bouncing. The Mayor of Doncaster had sent out a request for back-up, after the witches had attempted to blackmail her to aid them. General Hayworth delegated the job to Hunter, who quickly called his team, plus another fifty soldiers and witch-hunters. It seemed an excessive number, but Hunter would rather be over-prepared than caught out-numbered.

They set out that very evening, Hunter transporting them all in a blink, rather than wasting precious fuel. They arrived in Campsall Woods and set up camp. The information the Mayor had given them was that the witches were stationed in the nearby Brodsworth Hall.

James moved about the camp, making sure that no one was feeling too faint after blinking over here. He then made his way over to where Hunter and the rest of his team waited. They were poring over a map with a Sergeant O'Hara.

"I remember camping up here as a kid." James said, nodding at their map. "The trees will offer plenty of coverage, and we have the advantage of higher ground."

Hunter nodded, knowing that here was as good as anywhere. "We'll stay here tonight. It seems the safest option. O'Hara – send scouts on a five-mile radius. No one should know we're here, but I want to be sure. My team will take first watch."

"Yes sir." O'Hara moved away from the meeting, to find his second-in-charge.

"Trust the witches to get the first-class accommodation, while we're in tents." Alannah muttered.

"Well, at least we're not doing this in winter." Maria replied. "We'd freeze our arses off."

Alannah elbowed her in the ribs. "You wouldn't freeze. You've got someone to cuddle into."

James smirked at the comment. "Come on, Alannah. If you were desperate for a cuddle, I'm sure Hunter or Ian would oblige."

Hunter folded up the map and tucked it away. "Of course. If the alternative was hypothermia, I would definitely share body heat."

Alannah's cheeks flushed red as the rest of the team laughed. "That's the most romantic thing you've ever said to me, Hunter."

Hunter walked past her towards the tents, pausing to ruffle her hair in a very brotherly way. "I try my best."

Alannah squeaked, and ducked away from him, then flattened her hair again. She looked to the other three that were looking very amused. She shook her head. "No comment."

It was nearly the end of the first watch and Hunter sat nursing a hot drink as he stared down the hill. His mind was running over the smooth running of his team. They'd been working together for nearly a year and a half, and Hunter had to confess that he depended on them now. He didn't want anything complicating their unity. James and Maria were strong, and they seemed stronger together. Hunter marvelled that James had not done anything yet to cock things up. Or perhaps Maria was just very forgiving.

It had not passed Hunter by, that Alannah was becoming a little more insistent in her hints. Did the little Welsh girl expect him to sweep her up in his arms? Hunter didn't want to give thought to where Alannah's fantasies led, he was not going to indulge them. Perhaps he should get Maria to have a quiet word and persuade the girl to look elsewhere.

Hunter drummed his fingers on the tin cup of now lukewarm tea. When did this happen? A few years ago, he would have enjoyed the attention. She was a pretty girl - they could have flirted, possibly slept together, and entertained some short-lived relationship. Hunter blamed Sophie, it had to be her fault. Or was it because he was a father – did that automatically make you mature and responsible?

Adam was going to be a year old at the end of summer. A year old, and Hunter still wouldn't have seen his son.

He wondered if he looked like him, or did he take after his mother?

Hunter thought back to the conversation he'd had with James, the night he had learnt of Adam's birth, that they would wrap all this up and then claim his son. It had seemed an easy promise to make then, but nearly a year on, and they were no closer to their aim.

Hunter's thoughts stopped mid-track. Something didn't feel right. He checked his shields, finding them all intact, then sent his senses further down the wooded slope. Nothing, there was no- Hunter froze. There was movement in the woods, but camouflaged in such a way that Hunter could barely perceive it. He stood up, barely breathing as he tracked the faint whisper of life that moved up the hill, still hidden to his normal senses.

Hunter swore and ran back to the tents. It was only ten in the evening, and most were still at least half-awake.

"Ambush." He warned in a stony voice, quickly getting the attention of those in the campsite. "I don't know how many, coming up the hill. Get everyone ready for my signal."

The witch-hunters and soldiers moved without question, to follow his orders.

Hunter moved to the edge of camp and crouched in the darkness. He felt a pang of unease, that this was going to go terribly wrong. He closed his eyes and tried to sense the magic that was being used to cloak the witches. It was very subtle, by a very adept witch, but it didn't have the same feel as Sophie's magic. Hunter guessed that she had no part in this, but for some reason that did little to comfort him.

The witches were near impossible to perceive, and as Hunter waited to call for the counter-ambush, he heard the sudden cry of one of his men, taken out by an invisible enemy that had moved up the hill faster than Hunter had anticipated.

Hunter ignored the following outburst of cursing and gunshots, knowing that his men were fighting blind, he concentrated instead on breaking through the magic that disguised the witches. He grimaced at the skill of the caster; their spell seemed infallible. But then Hunter found a crack the breadth of a spider's web. He pushed the weak link until the spell faltered and broke. Suddenly the enemy was clear before their eyes again.

There was a rallying shout from the witch-hunters and soldiers as they pressed their new advantage.

Hunter heard a stuttered moan and heavy breathing beside him. James lay slumped on the ground by his feet, a trickle of blood starting to roll down from his mouth. Hunter swore, and knelt down beside him, throwing up a shield about them.

"James... what...?"

"Couldn't see... I couldn't see them. B-but had to defend you." James mumbled, then winced.

Hunter took in his surroundings and noticed two inert bodies lying nearby. He hadn't even noticed them approach, he'd been so focused on breaking the spell. He didn't know whether the two witches were dead yet, but that was the least of his worries right now.

"Come on, I'll get you to the first-aid tent." Hunter muttered, frustrated at his friend's heroism.

He moved to pick James up, but James just cried in pain, and pushed him away.

"Don't. It hurts, you bastard." James spat, then closed his eyes. "T-tell my family they should be proud of me. And Maria, tell Maria..."

Hunter felt the distracting attack along the lines of his shield and mentally shoved it away as though it were a mild irritant.

"Why are you talking like this? You're going to be fine. We'll finish up here, then get you patched up." Hunter said firmly.

"Need a bloody big patch." James laughed, his eyes straining at the effort, and his teeth stained red. He lifted his hand from his torso – his dark jumper looked damp, but deceptive – only on the pale flesh of his hand did the true extent of his blood loss show. "They hit me hard mate. Too hard even... even for you to fix."

James spoke calmly enough, only a groan of pain puncturing his control. James reached out and suddenly grabbed Hunter's arm with a bloodied hand. "I - I need to tell you..."

Hunter pushed him back down, desperate that he should rest and conserve his energy. "You can tell me after the battle."

"No... now." James growled weakly, as his skin paled, and sweat mingled with the blood on his brow.

"I don't blame you for any of this – I don't regret any of this. Except dying maybe." James smiled and laughed at his own useless joke. "I trusted Sophie too."

Hunter shook his head. He again felt magic attack his shield, and again he repulsed it. He was not listening to his best friend's final words, because James was not going to die, he could not die.

Hunter closed his eyes, trying to find something, that spark that made him different, that magic. He had done things people considered miracles, was it so hard to believe that he might be able to heal a simple wound? His powers always showed themselves when Hunter was at his greatest need – this time definitely counted.

"Please." Hunter whispered.

James' grip loosened on his arm and fell limply to his side. Hunter opened his eyes in time to witness the last breath leave his body. Hunter stared, frozen. He felt that if he even breathed, the world would shatter. But his emotions were beyond his control. He felt the anger and grief roil inside him, making his limbs quiver with excess energy, a demand that needed to be sated.

Hunter blacked out.

When he came to, Sergeant O'Hara had gently placed a hand on his shoulder, making Hunter jump. Hunter was still kneeling over James' body. Obviously only his mind had blacked out, his body was still working fine. He looked up at the soldier, who in turn looked warily back.

"What happened?" The man asked.

Hunter blinked, his mind slow and uncomprehending. "What do you mean?"

O'Hara pulled back his hand, looking quite scared. "Well sir, one minute we're being attacked by an enemy we can't see. Then we see them, but they couldn't touch us, and then – well just look at it, sir."

Hunter frowned, looking past the soldier. Even in the dark, Hunter's eyes were sharp, he could see the rest of his team moving cautiously across the open towards him – the open! The moon shone down onto a ravaged scene, the trees torn up by their roots, or blasted where they stood.

"Casualties?" Hunter asked weakly.

"Five on our side from when the battle began." The soldier reported. "We're still checking, but so far we haven't found any surviving witches."

Hunter took a deep breath. No surviving witches. The scene echoed back to the only other time Hunter had felt such a release of rage. But that had been in a church, the night Charlotte was killed.

"James? James!" Alannah's voice pierced his thoughts.

There was the added noise of footsteps now hurrying in his direction. Hunter didn't even bother looking up, as the rest of his team descended on them.

Chapter Twenty-four

Hunter did not sleep that night. His limbs were still filled with the restless energy of his grief. Which meant that he had dug a grave in the early hours of the morning, and by dawn, his team held a tearful burial.

Sergeant O'Hara stood with them to pay his respects.

Hunter stood there, unable to process any thought or feeling. Alannah clung to Maria's arm, her face streaked with tears, whereas Maria seemed to be experiencing the same numbness that was affecting Hunter. Ian stood next to Maria, his hand on her shoulder; he looked over to Hunter, the older man uncertain for once, of what to do.

Hunter let out a rattling breath and eventually moved away from the graveside, his legs just about working, though they felt like lead. He motioned for O'Hara to join him.

"We need to get moving. Send the men and women back to Manchester the mundane way. Also, can you organise an investigation into this – no one knew that we were here, save the Mayor. I want to know if she is implicated, or someone in her office has betrayed us. If it is possible, take our fallen back to their families."

"Yes sir." O'Hara answered automatically, then hesitated. "Sir, this does not have to be done now, if you need-"

"Sergeant. I-" Hunter interrupted, but stopped, looking back to his team that still huddled by the grave. It was impossible to think that James simply wouldn't be there anymore. It didn't make sense. But at least he was buried in his hometown. It's what he would have wanted. Now there was the monumental task of telling his family. Hunter's insides froze at the mere thought of the emotions and distress that he would be causing good people. People that had always welcomed him and treated Hunter as an extended part of the family.

"Sergeant, can you please inform James' uncle and aunt – I can provide you with an address, they don't live far from here."

Sergeant O'Hara frowned, obviously not comfortable being the bearer of bad news, and probably wondering why the best friend did not take the message.

Hunter saw the look and winced. "I cannot go, I cannot be the one to tell them. You have to understand; I am the one that dragged James into this world. Without me, he would have lived a normal, boringly safe life. It- it's my fault."

Hunter took a deep breath and moved away from O'Hara. He drifted closer to his team again. He had to get them back to Manchester, get them out of his charge and custody, so he could be selfish and grieve.

*****

"Where are we?" Alannah asked, confusion in her weary voice.

It was dark, the weak sunlight blocked by drapes.

153

Hunter took a deep breath; the very air was familiar and comforting. He easily navigated the chairs and low table and pulled back the heavy curtains.

"Astley Manor." He murmured, then shook his head. "Sorry, I wasn't concentrating."

Alannah moved closer to him, slipping her delicate hand into his. "It's ok."

Hunter wanted to express some gratefulness, but he couldn't even squeeze her hand, or raise the corner of his mouth in a grim smile. He just stared across the room, unfocussed, waiting to feel normal.

Ian coughed. "I'll let Mrs Astley and Charles know we're here."

He shot a concerned look at Maria, who hadn't said a word since last night, then left to find the other occupants of this house.

"I should…" Hunter broke off, not sure what he was going to say. He felt that he needed to do something, unused energy still burnt through his muscles, even as they felt like lead. But what could he do, he had already killed the witches and had his revenge. Should he go after their leader, should he face the Shadow Witch and take his anger out on her?

A life for a life. He had spared her, now James was dead.

There was a tug on his hand.

"Come to the kitchen." Alannah insisted. "You too, Maria. I'll make tea, then find something for us to eat."

Hunter glanced down at Alannah, the green of her eyes even brighter against the redness from crying. He nodded and allowed the girl to lead him to the kitchen.

Maria wrapped her arms protectively about her own chest, and silently followed.

It must have been the very early hours of the following morning, yet Hunter lay wide awake. He turned over again, sleep eluding him.

He didn't even have to close his eyes for the battle to play over and over, the pictures bright and bloody.

Hunter told himself that he knew – they all knew – that fighting meant the chance they might die. Hunter accepted that. But to lose someone else?

Hunter shuddered at the memory of the shattered forest, the energy that had boiled within himself. He had only ever experienced it once before, when the witches had killed Charlotte, his closest friend, save James.

Was that why the witches had done it? Had they wanted to – to defuse him? Sophie would have known that after Charlotte, only James could evoke such a reaction. Hunter thought bitterly that, once upon a time, the same could have been said for Sophie, herself.

Had she targeted him?

Hunter threw the cover away and got out of bed. Hardly thinking about what he was doing, he grabbed his dressing gown to cover the bare chest and boxers he had slept in – or tried to sleep in.

Hunter made his way down the silent corridor, until he got to a certain room. He took a deep breath and pushed open the door, stepping inside.

He wasn't sure what he was hoping to see. Perhaps a pair of glasses on the side-table, or an open book on the desk. But it was disappointingly tidy. Charles must have cleaned the room since the last time they came to stay – there was no hint of James left.

Hunter let out a breath he didn't know he was holding, when he heard a sob in the dark room. Hunter shuffled further into the room, to see Maria huddled in the shadow of the foot of the bed.

"Maria?" He said, but even his soft voice was startlingly loud.

Maria snapped her head in his direction. "Hunter." She hiccupped, fiercely wiping tears from her cheeks.

Hunter stood, uncertain as ever in the face of emotion. "You ok?" He asked, inwardly wincing at the pointless words.

"Yeah..." Maria coughed to kick the waver out of her voice. "I... I know I shouldn't be in here, but I – I-"

As she broke off, Hunter heard her breath hitch as she tried to control herself.

"Shh, it's fine." Hunter replied, stepping closer, then sliding down to sit next to her.

Maria groaned, and wiped her eyes again. "You know, this is the first time I've cried since my dad died, twelve years ago. I don't do crying; I don't do emotion."

Hunter guessed this was one of those times it was best to stay quiet and let Maria vent. He leant his shoulder against hers, but otherwise said nothing.

"Not when I lost friends in Afghanistan. Not when my husband left me." Maria sighed. "You know, you get in the habit of not feeling, not connecting."

Maria drew her knees up, hugging them to her chest. "But James was... unexpected. I don't even know when I fell for him. And I never got a chance to – to tell him..."

Maria broke off in a sob. Hunter put his arm reassuringly about her shoulders. "It's ok. He knew, he-" Hunter paused to steady his voice. "He knew, and he loved you too."

Maria huffed, and shoved him with her elbow. "You're lying, you're just saying that to make me feel better." She said, but couldn't hide her smile through her tears.

Hunter shrugged. "I've known James for years; I've never seen him look at anyone the way he looked at you. Plus, you're the only woman he's ever taken home to meet his family."

Maria leant her head against Hunter's shoulder. "I hardly knew him. I was foolish enough to think that we'd have forever. I'd give anything to have just one more day with him."

Hunter closed his eyes, tears leaking out the corners of them. "Me too."

Maria sighed, wiping her eyes on her pyjama sleeve. "I don't suppose time travel is one of your tricks."

Hunter grunted. "No. At least, I don't think it is." Hunter gazed at the dark ceiling, he hated to admit that he honestly could not say for sure. He felt anew the gaping hole in his knowledge. Should he have done what James once requested – sought the traces of the Benandanti instead of fighting the witches?

They sat like that for what must have been an hour. Maria had grown so still that Hunter thought she must have drifted to sleep.

"So, what now?" She suddenly asked.

"What now, what?" Hunter repeated groggily.

"I mean, what's going to happen next? We can't stay at this stalemate."

Hunter sighed. "Next, we force the witches into battle, and we kill them."

There was a pause, before Maria dared to ask a burning question. "Including Sophie?"

Hunter grimaced. "Sophie Murphy has ceased to exist. The Shadow Witch has killed James, and countless others. There can be no forgiveness."

Chapter Twenty-five

The next morning, after Charles had force fed them all a hearty breakfast, Hunter assembled with his diminished team to return to headquarters.

When they blinked into the secure compound, a few of the newer recruits jumped at their sudden appearance, but the rest seemed to accept that four people had appeared out of thin air. It was amazing how 'normal' they considered Hunter's new-found skill, and if Hunter had been in the mood for it, he would have felt relief. It had not been long ago he had feared being outcast – or worse, killed – for his magic-like abilities.

Hunter led the way to the Council's makeshift meeting room, where his team settled in. They waited in gloomy silence, nothing to be said.

Eventually the door opened, and General Hayworth marched in, a look of relief crossing his face when he saw them.

"Sergeant O'Hara explained what happened. I had hoped only grief delayed you, but I was worried the rest of you had another run in…" The General paused for breath.

159

"You couldn't have bloody sent word that you were fine, and took a detour, could you?!"

A delicate hand reached out, cautioning him, as Nadira Shah came in beside him. "Now General, there's little point berating them over what has already happened. They are back, that's what matters."

As she turned to face the others, her beautiful brown eyes were filled with sincerity and sadness. "I am sorry for your loss. I have never heard anything but high praise for James Bennett."

Hunter looked down at the table before him. He knew that Nadira meant well, but every time he lost someone, he knew the words wouldn't help

"Thank you, ma'am." Ian's voice rang out, speaking for the first time today.

"Alright." Hayworth started gruffly. "On with business. I daresay we all need the distraction."

Nadira drifted to the meeting table and sat down, indicating that the others should join her. "While you were gone, the Council has been discussing our next step."

"I hope it involves killing a lot of witches." Alannah bitterly interjected.

Nadira smiled compassionately in the young girl's direction. "We cannot go on as we are, allowing them to pick us off one by one. We need to face them in a place of our choosing, for once. We need to bring them to battle."

"So, they can pick us off en masse." Ian added darkly.

General Hayworth shot him a warning look. "Not so. Our intelligence tells us that we have the greater numbers now. With Hunter to block their magic, our numbers will overwhelm theirs, just like Little Hanting."

Hunter felt uneasiness knot in his stomach, but he pushed it aside. This was what he wanted, what he needed. An end to it all, and revenge for James, for Anthony Marks, Charlotte King, Brian Lloyd…

"When and where?" He asked.

"Three weeks should be enough time to rally the troops, everyone is keen to make this stand."

"Three weeks."

"We need to hit them before the summer solstice." Nadira confirmed. "We don't want to risk them channelling its power for their next offensive."

"The 'where' is Salisbury Plains. I've had men down there for months, salvaging equipment. They've even got a tank working."

"Will a tank be enough to kill the Shadow?" Alannah asked warily, remembering their last encounter with her.

Hayworth made a noncommittal gesture. "I really hope so; we've got nothing stronger."

"Magic isn't about strength." Hunter muttered. Magic often manifested in the physical, but that didn't mean brawn alone could defeat it. On the other hand, Hunter couldn't imagine anything surviving a few mortar rounds.

"Fine. So, what are our orders, General?" Hunter eventually asked, doing his best to appear contrite.

Hayworth exchanged a look with Nadira. "We appreciate everything you've done, but in view of your loss, we think you should all take leave until the battle."

Hayworth was met with four very disbelieving faces.

"You want your best team to sit and twiddle their thumbs?" Maria snapped, finally breaking out of her miserable silence.

"You all need time to recover and come to terms with James' death. We cannot trust your judgement in the field at this time." Nadira said firmly.

Hunter leant back in his chair, observing the two leaders. So, they were worried that he and his team would crack, or act rashly. Huh, they might have a point.

Hunter pushed back his chair, the legs scraping across the wooden floor. Without a word, he stood up and walked out of the meeting room.

*****

Half an hour later, Ian came to find him. Hunter was working out his frustration in the gym, with a punch bag. His feet moved half-heartedly, but he threw his whole weight behind each punch.

"Hey, want to spar?" Ian called, breaking Hunter's rhythm.

Hunter stopped, glancing up at the intruder. "Not really, Ian, no."

"I'll go easy on you." Ian offered.

Hunter sighed and backed away, the punch bag having lost its appeal, with Ian providing distraction. Hunter sat down on the closest bench.

"You ok?" Ian asked.

Hunter rolled his shoulders to loosen them up. "I'm fine." He snapped.

"Uh-huh." Ian sat down on the bench beside him. "And truthfully?"

"I'm… I'm good enough, I don't need the Council thinking I need mollycoddling." Hunter threw his arm out in the vague direction of the Council's offices.

"They're just worried about you." Ian replied.

Hunter snorted. "They're worried what I might do, I am the freak of nature and breeding, after all."

Ian crossed his arms, his patience for the snarky comments from the younger man running lower than

162

normal today. "No, they care for you, and they're worried because you lost your best friend."

Hunter stood up again, feeling restless energy through his limbs again. He paced to the punch bag and back. "Don't pretend that you know how I'm feeling right now, Ian."

Ian stood up so quickly, that Hunter froze mid-step. "Don't presume you have monopoly on grief right now Hunter. I may not have known James as long as you, but you will not trivialise my friendship with him."

Hunter backed off a little, he'd never seen Ian show emotion, nor speak so strongly. It just added to his guilt that waited impatiently to kick in.

"I'm sorry." Hunter mumbled, sitting down again.

They sat in silence for a minute, before Ian finally spoke. "So, are you going to follow orders this time, or did you have some plan concocted?"

Hunter shrugged. "I hadn't actually gotten that far yet."

Hunter ran over his initial desire to kill as many witches as possible. Was it best to take out their leader, instead? Once they had lost their Shadow Witch, would the rest crumble.

"It did occur to me that a small team could slip through their defences and overcome the Shadow Witch." Hunter admitted.

Ian nodded. "Ok, but what then? We couldn't kill her last time, what makes you think we could be any more successful this time."

Unfortunately, the sergeant had a point. But what if they didn't kill her, or not immediately so. "We could bind her."

"You might want to clarify what you mean by that." Ian replied with a chuckle.

"We used to bind witches that surrendered. Using an amulet, you can bind their power from them, rendering them harmless – or at least, as harmless as any human." Hunter explained. "If we could get to Sophie, distract her and bind her, she'd be powerless."

Ian nodded again. "Ok, sounds plausible. We've only got to subdue her; that should be... interesting. You know, the best distraction will be an army with tanks."

Hunter's shoulders dropped. "You want me to wait, too."

"Whatever you decide, I'll be there with you. So will Alannah and Maria. But it's just three more weeks to wait, and we can go in with the army at our backs."

"Waiting three weeks is as impossible a task as overcoming the Shadow Witch." Hunter muttered.

Ian clapped him on the shoulder. "Good, I knew that you'd see things my way. Now, do you think you can find one of those binding amulet thingies?"

Hunter was about to remark that that was James' job. But he settled for a silent nod.

Chapter Twenty-six

A fortnight before the summer solstice, Hunter began to transport the troops that had been gathering at Manchester, taking them down to the abandoned village of Imber, which served as a temporary place to regroup.

Witch-hunters from all over the UK made their own way there, having gotten the message that the MMC was finally making a stand. Hunter watched as the numbers on Salisbury Plain swelled. Most of them were military, the number of surviving witch-hunters was depressingly low – a few hundred, no more.

Hunter greeted those he knew, seeing the same determination in each face that they would finally put this world right, they would finally get revenge for their lost friends and colleagues. There were a few missing faces that Hunter had yet to see, he hoped they had just been delayed, but there was no one from the Newcastle branch here. But his concern for Toby and the others had to be put aside as the chaos of their army had to be organised.

Hunter pushed through the crowd to one of the houses that had been set aside for those in command. Recognising him, the soldiers guarding the door let him through.

Hunter saw the familiar faces of General Hayworth, Nadira Shah and Sergeant Dawkins. There were also the less familiar faces of the regional leaders. They gave Hunter a curious look when he entered, obviously intrigued by the famous 7th gen that had been flitting about the country.

"Any sign of Jonathan and the wiccans?" Nadira asked.

"No, ma'am. But it's still early." Hunter answered.

Nadira looked troubled. "They promised they would come."

Hunter frowned, he had gradually begun to trust Jonathan, and had started to take him seriously; it would be shame if he let them down now.

"They're only wiccans." One of the other witch-hunters voiced. "Are they really so important, if they cannot fight?"

Nadira turned her brown eyes in the direction of the one that spoke, until he dropped his gaze, ashamedly. "They have been an important ally to us all. They cannot fight, nor do harm, but they have been trying to emulate the shield Hunter creates, with some success. They might just save your skin tomorrow."

Hunter tried to look as though this was not news to him, but he was as shocked as the rest of the room. Was that why Jonathan had quizzed him about his powers, whenever he got chance? Hunter had thought it mere curiosity.

"That's ah, very good news." The witch-hunter replied, sounding much more contrite. "Why did you not share it sooner?"

"We have kept their attempts secret; we did not want the witches to target the wiccans." Nadira met the eye of each and every person. "It is still early days and in the experimental stages. But our needs are at their greatest, now."

"So, does everyone know their role tomorrow?" General Hayworth asked.

There was a chorus of confirmation. This would all be over tomorrow, the main body would await the witches in the centre of the Plains; two groups would keep hidden to the east and west, attempting to catch the witches from as many angles as possible. A select group was in charge of the military vehicles and heavy artillery.

And Hunter? No one had given him an outright order; it was assumed that he would go where he was most needed. Hunter had the feeling that the General knew that he intended to tackle the Shadow Witch and was simply turning a blind eye.

"Well then, tomorrow at 0600 we will move into position." General Hayworth said. "Our spies will make sure the message gets to the witches – we can expect them tomorrow, the day after at the latest."

****

The witch-hunters and their allies amassed on the Plains, making a defiant stand. Hunter had walked amongst them and had been comforted by their numbers. But when he blinked away to the copse that hid another portion of their fighters, he looked back and saw their army dwarfed by the expanse of the rolling Plains. A knot of anxiety tightened in his stomach, knowing that others were watching and judging his confidence in this endeavour.

Were they brave, or just mad, to pit themselves against the greatest magical threat in centuries?

Hunter thought over the event ahead. He would need all of his team when tackling the Shadow Witch. The potentially impossible task of killing her might be easier

167

than distracting her and subduing her long enough for Hunter to use the amulet to bind her.

He put his hand in his pocket, wrapping his fingers about the black silk ribbon, and smooth opal stone. Hunter had had to rummage through some dusty boxes in Manchester to find an item he thought would be strong enough. The smooth curves of the stone were supposed to make it a strong reservoir of power, and this type had never failed him before.

It was a pretty commonly used tool for binding witches. Or at least it had been – as far as Hunter was aware, no witch had been bound since the rebellion. Now, it was kill or be killed.

Quickly bored of waiting for the witches to arrive, Hunter flitted between the groups, checking for news and acting as messenger for those in charge. He watched as the men and women slowly lost the look of anxiety and determination, and as the day wore on, they set up casual groups to share food.

Those in charge kept a positive and controlled look, but to Hunter they all grumbled over the same thing.

"Hayworth said today."

As evening drew in, Hunter went to find General Hayworth for the fifth time that day.

"Anything new to report?" The General asked.

Hunter shook his head. "No sir. Only that everyone is wondering where our enemy is, and why they're taking so damned long."

The General sighed, gazing out across his troops, intuitively knowing they were all thinking likewise. "It has been the witches' habit, to date, to run in when provoked and to be ruled by haste and passion. We will give them another twenty-four hours, and then question whether they are up to something more devious."

There were many remarks that Hunter wanted to give, but he just bowed his head and retired to where his friends were setting up camp.

*****

The following morning, dawn rose on the impatiently waiting army. It had been a restless night, with those not on watch hardly daring to sleep, for fear of a night-time attack.

Hunter didn't think he'd slept at all, and as soon as it was a socially acceptable time, he began to repeat his rounds of the different camps. The summer night had been mild, and most people were in a positive mood.

Time slowly ticked by, and after midday, Hunter sought the General. For once, even he looked disappointed.

"I wish I knew what devilry they're up to." General Hayworth muttered as Hunter approached. They stood side by side, looking out to the hazy, summer horizon.

"There's still no sign of the wiccans." Hunter commented.

Hayworth sighed. "That doesn't make me feel any better. I never pegged Jonathan as a coward."

"Toby Robson and the rest of the Newcastle branch haven't arrived, either." Hunter added.

The General looked towards Hunter; his expression troubled.

"I could go, search for foul play." Hunter offered, it did not cross his mind for a moment that Toby or Jonathan were playing the coward. The rest of the groups of witch-hunters and wiccans were questionable.

Hayworth thought about it, but eventually shook his head. "No, I need you here. I can't risk you getting delayed or caught up when the witches hit here."

Hunter bit his tongue, knowing that any comment he made about this long wait had already been said.

Chapter Twenty-seven

It had gone 9pm and the long summer evening was finally starting to darken. The gathered witch-hunters and soldiers settled in for another night out on the Plains. It had been deemed illogical to move them before morning. They would go back to their designated bases, ready to re-group when a new plan of action had been determined.

Hunter sat in silence with Maria, watching the sun set. There was no need to speak, just sitting there was enough. As the sun dropped below the horizon, leaving the darkening sky streaked with red, Hunter felt a familiar warmth burn through his jacket pocket. He pulled the wiccan stone out, to see it glowing bright with warning. It had become such habit to carry it, Hunter had not thought twice by pocketing it.

Not understanding the message behind this basic rock, he looked up to see that several others had gotten to their feet, holding out stones and looking as bemused as he.

"They're coming!" A distant cry rang out. "They're coming!"

The shout was taken up across the army, and there was a hive of activity to kit up.

Hunter scanned the dim horizon, until he found a patch of darkness that was so thick that even his eyes could not make sense of it.

Out of that darkness came the movement of figures. They came out in ones and twos, then tens and hundreds.

Hunter quickly pushed through the gathered witch-hunters and soldiers, to get to the forefront. He was vaguely aware of Maria following him, and the familiar, broad-shouldered figure of Ian joining them.

The witches amassed on the grey horizon, their numbers spreading out and standing ready.

Hunter's sharp eyes picked out one stepping forward with achingly familiar movements. The Shadow Witch turned her gaze across her enemies, trying to pick out the leaders.

"I give you this chance to surrender." Sophie's voice rang out across the expectant quiet. "The witchkind have won, your allies are destroyed, and you are all that remains of the resistance to the new world."

The army stood as one, silent and unmoving to this offer.

"So stubborn." Sophie continued, when it was clear that none would respond. "A demonstration then."

With a wave of her hand, two male witches dragged a man forward. Hunter gritted his teeth as he recognised their prisoner. Jonathan.

The usually calm and collected wiccan looked panicked as he was thrown at the Shadow Witch's feet. His hands were bound, and his face was bloody, eyes black and swollen from his treatment.

Hunter's gut twisted at the thought of what the man had suffered.

172

"You fight against magic." The Shadow Witch shouted. "But are hypocrites that use it as and when you need. Not only is one among your number as guilty of magic as I…"

Hunter felt more than one set of eyes turn in his direction, but he held back the need to wince as his enemy continued.

"…but you ally yourselves with wiccans – parasites who cling to magic." Sophie looked down at Jonathan with clear distaste. "I don't know whether to be disgusted or insulted, that you would plan to overcome us with these – these…"

Sophie's lip curled as she failed to find the words to express herself adequately. Oh well, actions always spoke louder than words. She took a step back, and with an idle flick of her hand, the two male witches cast the spell they were forming.

There was a flash of light and a piercing scream, as flames engulfed Jonathan. The sound of his pain rolled over the Plains and made the assembled army stir. Hunter felt bile rising in his throat, but before he could do anything, Jonathan's screams were cut off by a single gunshot. The wiccan slumped, lifeless to the ground.

Hunter glanced to his side and saw Maria slowly lowering her gun, pale but calm. Unable to speak, he simply nodded. They couldn't save their friend, but they could cut short his suffering.

On some unspoken signal, the two armies charged.

Hunter felt the swell of magic, and his own power respond, throwing up a shield that was soon hammered under the weight of hundreds of witches. His movements were slow, as he focused on maintaining it, while keeping his gun steady on the next witch in his eye line. Things were quickly dissolving into chaos.

Hunter shouted for Alannah; his voice lost in the melee. His eyes tore from one struggling fighter to the next, his heart pounding with exertion and fear.

Ian grabbed his shoulder. "There!" He pointed.

Hunter allowed himself to feel relief as he spotted the fourth member of his team making her way towards them. The young Welsh girl held her side and limped slightly, blood stained her cheek and arm, but otherwise she was fine.

She looked around the group, her green eyes bright. "Well, what are we waiting for?"

"Come on then." Ian stated. "Let's make this bitch mortal."

Ian turned and led the way, his bulky form pushing a path through the battleground. Maria followed him.

Hunter made to follow them, but Alannah caught his arm.

"What's wrong?"

Alannah looked up at him with determination. For an answer, she moved onto her toes. Her hands locked behind Hunter's neck and she pulled him down to her.

Hunter was more than a little surprised at the kiss but didn't pull back as her lips caught his gently. When Alannah let him go, Hunter straightened again.

"Alannah…"

Alannah shook her head. "I didn't want to go into this with any regrets."

Hunter glanced about, checking for immediate danger; now was not the time for this. "Alannah, we'll talk after the battle."

Hunter grabbed her hand and dragged her with him before she could oppose. He was glad there was an important battle to deal with before he had to have that talk with Alannah. She was a friend, and a little sister to him now.

When they caught up with the others, Ian gave them an odd, concerned look; at which Hunter realised he was still holding Alannah's hand, and guiltily dropped it.

The four of them fought their way through another line of witches, leaving their opponents dead or incapacitated as they pushed on to the next clearing.

Hunter had a feeling of déjà vu as he saw Sophie standing alone, her power rolling off her. With a single breath, he felt his own anti-magic stir and react with hers. A dome of energy spread out in a shimmer of colour against the dark night. Sophie immediately detected the source, and her furious hazel eyes snapped onto Hunter.

"So, you've brought an extra friend this time?" Her eyes flicked across the rest of his team.

Hunter's jaw tensed, there was nothing to be said to this woman that had played him for a fool, while killing those closest to him. Alannah noticed his mood, and supportively squeezed his arm.

Sophie noticed the gesture, and her eyes snapped to the Welsh girl. "You again."

Alannah flashed Hunter a smile, then turned to the witch. "Yes, me." She confirmed. Then attacked.

Chapter Twenty-eight

Alannah's knife glanced off the Shadow Witch's arm, the cut healing as soon as it was inflicted.

Sophie snarled in pain and her hand shot out, taking the opportunity to grab Alannah by the neck. Her fingers closed tighter.

"He'll never be yours." She hissed at the little Welsh girl, jealous eyes flicking to Hunter.

Alannah scratched at Sophie's iron hold, starting to choke. "Wanna bet?" She gasped.

Sophie leant in closer, her expression of fury suddenly changing to shock as she felt two arms encircle her and pin her in place. She instinctively struggled, but the arms just tightened.

Alannah broke free, and fell to her knees, gulping in precious air. Hunter rushed to her side.

"You said distract her." She croaked.

"Not by using yourself as bait." He growled, furious at her crazy move.

"Hunter!"

Hunter looked up at Maria's shout, to see the lieutenant aiming her gun steadily at Sophie's head. Oh yes, there was something to do. He pulled the opal stone amulet and black silk from his pocket and stepped closer to Sophie. Her hazel eyes locked on the items and immediately grew wide, she began to struggle in earnest against Ian's hold, but with little effect.

Hunter hurried to press the amulet against her hand and bound it with the black ribbon. Sophie shrieked as she felt her power sapped by the ritual, the opal glowing with the strength of the power it absorbed.

Hunter stepped back, nodding to Ian, who released his prisoner from his grip. Maria's aim followed the witch as she dropped to the ground, shivering. Hunter felt the magic in the air suddenly lessen and he looked at his enemy, so weak upon her knees.

"What have you done?" Sophie demanded.

"What needed to be done." Hunter replied. "Surrender now, and you will be charged for your crimes. Or, by the Malleus Maleficarum, I am empowered to take the necessary measures."

Sophie narrowed her eyes in his direction – that he should give her the formal spiel!

Before she could reply, another wave of pain shot through her, knocking her flat on her back.

"What's happening?" Alannah asked, as she pulled herself to her feet. Even though she was a young witch-hunter, she could see this wasn't going normally. The Shadow Witch writhed in pain, and the amulet still glowed – in fact it was getting brighter than when Hunter had performed the ritual.

Alannah stepped forward to inspect the amulet more closely.

Without warning, the world was dissolved in a bright flash, as the amulet exploded.

Hunter came to, aware of movement around him, but the sound sluggish. The next thing he was aware of was that he was flat on his back, and there was an immense pain resonating from his right shoulder and back.

Movement caught his eye, a figure stepped into his eye line, from the lack of military gear he guessed it to be a witch.

Hunter forced a painful breath into his lungs and let his eyes scout his surroundings. The night was lit by fire and spells, but he could tell little else.

Bracing himself for the shock of pain, Hunter pushed himself onto his side. His head throbbed with a migraine, as well as from the overwhelming magic in the area.

His ears began to hear again, starting with the curses of witches, their footsteps as they hurried back as they realised he was alive. He heard his name hissed by several voices but ignored them all.

Hunter focused on seeing the inert bodies nearby. He hoped that they had just been knocked out like him, but seeing Alannah's open, unseeing eyes, dropped a weight in his stomach.

Not wanting to think or feel, Hunter staggered to his feet. His eyes snapped onto Sophie, she became the only thing in focus, and he threw himself in her direction.

Sophie's hazel eyes widened at his approach and she threw up thick shadows about herself in defence.

Hunter ran forward, ignoring the spike of pain in his ribs and shoulder. He charged into the darkness. He felt a delicate hand touch his, followed by the familiar, disorientating warmth and nothingness that accompanied being transported by the Shadow Witch.

Hunter landed on cold, hard ground with a thud. He rolled onto his side and retched. He couldn't remember ever feeling so dizzy with pain. He cracked open his eyes to get his bearings. All he saw were a pair of feet in front of him.

His eyes travelled up, to see Sophie standing over him. She looked blood-stained and exhausted, much like how he felt. She sighed, seeing him regaining consciousness, and knelt beside him. Her lip curled at his weak struggles.

"You just can't admit defeat, can you?"

Sophie looked up, beyond him, to where Hunter could detect weak flashes of light.

"It's over." Sophie stated, gazing firmly back down at him.

Hunter felt the blackness at the edge of his senses sweep up and overwhelm him.

Chapter Twenty-nine

Hunter awoke – which in itself seemed like a major achievement. Sophie had not killed him, even when she had the perfect chance to. Hunter's head hurt to process any reason behind it, instead he focused on the simpler things.

It was light. With the low-hanging sun and cool air, Hunter sluggishly surmised that it was early morning.

He raised his head just enough to confirm that he was still on the Salisbury Plains. He could make out the deserted village that they had used, and the copse of trees their reinforcements had hidden within.

Hunter felt a stab of uneasiness. It was far too quiet.

He steeled himself to get to his feet. Hunter did not trust his ability to blink to the battleground, so made the slow and steady march to cover the distance.

There was no sign of life, only bodies laid strewn across the Plains. Hunter choked down the bile that threatened to rise.

Hunter gave the fleetest glances to each noting those he recognised. With each familiar face, his heart hardened. Now was not the time for grief. Instead he had to… to…

Hunter stopped in his tracks as he saw General Hayworth, such a steady source of leadership over the past couple of years. Now he lay with vicious burns on one side. But he had not gone down alone, the bodies of half a dozen witches were testament to his fight.

Hunter waited for the overwhelming power and blackout that had accompanied James' death, but he only felt numb.

Eventually he moved on again, further into the battlefield. There were less witch-hunters and soldiers here – proof of how far his team had successfully pushed through the witch ranks.

He saw three bodies ahead, and despite his nausea that begged for attention, his feet carried him mercilessly forward.

Hunter dropped to his knees as he struggled to breathe. The blast from the broken amulet had lifted them all off their feet. His friends had been killed in that moment. Sweet young Alannah; the dependable Ian; and Maria, who had never recovered from losing James. He had failed them all. They could never have guessed that trying to bind Sophie's powers could have such a result, in fact he remembered Sophie's look of surprise at the glowing, burning amulet. But Hunter could not forget that he had been the one to suggest this plan.

Hunter had no idea how he had survived the blast, he wished he had not.

Hunter lost track of how long he knelt there, the hot sun burning the back of his neck. His thoughts were struggling to connect, and his emotions had completely abandoned him.

They had been defeated.

Had anyone else survived? Surrounded by the dead, Hunter found it impossible to be optimistic.

What did he do now? What allies did he have left? He couldn't stay here; he was an easy target if the witches returned.

Hunter closed his eyes, letting his subconscious direct him as he blinked away from the battleground.

Despite it being the middle of summer, the air in the Manor was still cool.

Hunter looked down about the sitting room in which he had appeared, there were little signs everywhere of Mrs Astley and Charles' occupation of the house. Hunter thought about making his presence known but dismissed the idea. He moved into the hallway and made his way to towards the study, mindful of making as little noise as possible.

The Manor was quiet now. The last time he had been here his allies had filled the rooms. Their absence was painfully clear.

Once he entered the study, Hunter looked around. For all his books and records, it had all come to nothing. There had to be some answer – but not here.

He rummaged through his desk and pulled out paper and a pen.

'We are in dark days. I write this hurriedly at my desk, not knowing to whom I write, but wanting my story to be known. I hope it is found by one of my kind, and in turn gives hope…

My name is George Astley VII, known to my friends as Hunter...

... I am going to find the Benandanti.'

Hunter continued to scratch away, filling the paper with text, then folded the page when he finished. He had no idea who, if anyone, would read it; nor what help it might give, but it eased his anxiety and settled his course.

Taking one last look around, committing the room to memory, Hunter vanished.

Other books by K.S. Marsden:

Witch-Hunter ~ *now available in audiobook*
The Shadow Rises (Witch-Hunter #1)
The Shadow Reigns (Witch-Hunter #2)
The Shadow Falls (Witch-Hunter #3)

Witch-Hunter Prequels
James: Witch-Hunter (#0.5)
Sophie: Witch-Hunter (#0.5)
Kristen: Witch-Hunter (#2.5) ~ *coming 2020*

Enchena
The Lost Soul: Book 1 of Enchena
The Oracle: Book 2 of Enchena

Northern Witch
Winter Trials (Northern Witch #1)
Awaken (Northern Witch #2)
The Breaking (Northern Witch #3)

Read on for a preview of *The Shadow Falls*, the exciting finale to the Witch-Hunter trilogy.

A letter from our hero...

We are in dark days. I write this hurriedly at my desk, not knowing to whom I write, but wanting my story to be known. I hope it is found by one of my kind, and in turn gives hope...

My name is George Astley VII, known to my friends as Hunter. If it matters to you, I am 28 years old, English; and in a time of peace I would be the lord of Astley Manor, near the village of Little Hanting.

But this is not a time of peace, we have been fighting the losing side of a war for the past two years. Fighting against the witches. It all started when the legendary Shadow Witch arose - a witch whose magic was without limit, a witch raised to nurse a thousand years of insult and hatred. She plunged the world into darkness so that she and the other witch kind could claw above the stricken and powerless humans, preferably with as many casualties as possible to assuage their anger.

Where do I fit in with all this? In the very centre, shouldering both the blame and the hope.

I am a witch-hunter. As was my father, and his father and so on. I am the 7th generation of witch-hunters belonging to the organisation called the Malleus Maleficarum Council, which has successfully policed and hidden magic and witches for hundreds of years. Until now.

The Shadow Witch approached me in the guise of Sophie Murphy, a beautiful, intelligent woman that I thought was an innocent that I saved and sheltered from witches. With a grating stubbornness, Sophie demanded to join the MMC and train as a witch-hunter. I was the one that allowed her into our Council. I was the one that would let her learn all our secrets. I was the one that would later fall in love with her.

She finally revealed herself as the Shadow Witch, and the first of many battles between the witches and witch-hunters was fought, in which our side was nearly decimated.

What remained of the MMC regrouped, driven by desperation against this new and unbelievable force. We had only one advantage: the Shadow Witch revealed too much about the hidden talent born into witch-hunters - into me in particular. I don't know how I do it, I cannot explain it. Some liken my talents to magic, all I know is that I am strong enough to repel witches and protect those around me, amongst other useful skills. With my new skills, we initially managed to repel the Shadow Witch and destroy her followers. She seemed to vanish for the best part of a year and, as terrible and fierce as they were, we began to beat back the witches.

Then the Shadow Witch returned, stronger than ever, and even I was helpless in her path. She systematically destroyed the witch-hunters and their allies, returning power and victory to the witches in a devastating way. Those fateful days of battle will haunt me forever, as I watched brave men and women fall at my side.

There might be witch-hunters in hiding somewhere out there, but as far as I am aware, I am the only one left.

Friendless, alone, and the most wanted man alive, I've decided it's time to learn all I can about this mysterious power I have. I am going to find the Benandanti.

One

The small town was near deserted. Half the people had fled, or just plain vanished. The other half sat behind their locked doors, no one ventured out once the sun set. So, no one saw the sudden appearance of a man in the rough piazza.

One moment the square was empty, the next there he stood. He was tall, well-built and had perhaps been handsome, but now his clothes were creased, his face rugged, worn and wary, and half hidden by the short, dark beard and straggly black hair.

It was a very different image than the old, relatively carefree Hunter Astley. He'd been rich, good-looking and popular.

He'd been on the run for nearly eight months, ever since the last big battle in which the witch-hunters and their allies had finally been decimated. He hadn't dared stop anywhere for long, empty villages where no eyes could see him, or in the few dense cities that still existed where he could get lost in the crowd. He made his locations erratic and illogical, to throw off his hunters for a few peaceful hours.

Hunter had tried coming to Italy last summer, but found that wherever he went, the witches were close behind. Hunter didn't doubt that the Shadow Witch had a few spies permanently placed around here, for she knew how strongly Friuli would pull Hunter. For here was the region which had been the home to the Benandanti, centuries ago, the original anti-witches.

He eventually admitted defeat and fled to America, tracking down one lead in the library at Georgetown University; followed by Cornell, Glasgow and Ulster. All he found were teasers and hints to what he truly wished to know.

As winter came around, Hunter kept his movements in the southern hemisphere. It was easier and safer than trying to find warmth and shelter – he could put no one in such danger.

But finally, spring came again, and Hunter was drawn back to Friuli. If the modern equivalent of the Benandanti existed anywhere, it would be here. It was dangerous, but Hunter had to find them, he was out of options. He'd started at the northernmost edge of Friuli and searched each town and village for hope. This one was close to the Lago di Sauris, a large landmark that allowed Hunter to gain his bearings in his speedy method of travel.

Hunter strode up to the nearest house and banged sharply on the wooden door. Dogs started to bark, but there was no sound of people.

"Per favore. Please, I need help." Hunter called out; his voice rough from disuse.

He heard the soft pad of feet and the creak of shutters. Hunter stepped back and looked at the surrounding houses.

"Please." He repeated to the dark, empty street. "I'm not a witch, I just need help. I'm looking for some people. They used to live here, many years ago. They did magic, good magic. Please."

Hunter's voice trailed off, he was used to the suspicion and wariness that now ruled every person's life. It was the way of the world under the rule of the witches. If this town couldn't help him, he'd travel to the next, and the next, persisting in his search.

"We want no magic here, signor." A warning voice came from behind a crack in a shutter.

Hunter turned in the voice's direction. "No, I'm not here to harm you, and I'm not staying. But if you could help me by telling me anything, anything about the Benandanti…"

"I've never heard of them; they don't live here." The voice replied curtly.

Hunter frowned, it was a negative response, but at least someone was answering him - albeit through a blocked window.

"No, they might not live anywhere now. But they were in this region four hundred years ago."

"Four hundred years?" The voice spluttered. "Nobody here can help you, signor. It is too long ago. Now leave us in peace."

Hunter called out again, but got no response. He even banged on the reinforced shutters but only set the dogs off again. It had been briefly promising, but turned out to be less than helpful. Oh well, next village.

Hunter turned to leave the way he came when he suddenly stopped, seeing a pair of brown eyes peering around a crack in a door.

"Signor." A quiet woman's voice came. "It is true we know nothing, but try the Donili monks. They have a small monastery a few kilometres south-west of here."

The door clicked shut.

"Thank you. Grazie." Hunter said quietly to the still night air.

He hadn't gotten any answers - hell, he'd hardly managed to get any questions out, but this was a start, a thread to follow. Not bad, he reflected as he left the village. Even a place as small and unimportant as this was dangerous - this close to the Benandanti rumours, it was best to travel unmarked paths and camp alone and

192

unknown. Which meant hunkering down in the lonely forest that rose to the hills. Not a comfortable prospect, but at least the weather was mild.

At dawn Hunter was on his feet once more, set resolutely south-west, detouring only for the most stubborn natural barriers. The woman had said a few kilometres. A few. What an ill-defined description. She could mean three kilometres, while he considered it seven, or vice versa. And did she mean precisely south-west, or bearing more to the left or right? He might walk right past the home of the Donili monks, or not walk far enough. The dismal beat of his thoughts matched his steady footsteps.

He thought of the steps that had brought him here. He had thought of nothing but the Benandanti for months. The focus allowed him to block out the nightmare of last year; investigating every dusty book, every story and myth was preferable than facing the death and violence that was behind him.

The minutes seemed to drag by, and a mere hour pushing on exhausted him but Hunter didn't stop, the distance passed slowly but steadily. He kept a keen eye for any sign of a monastery, anything to show he was on track, but so far there had been nothing man-made, there had been no sight nor sou--

A scream pierced the peaceful countryside. Shouts followed and worse, laughter.

Hunter stopped. The sensible part of him warned caution, those screams could only mean trouble and he shouldn't endanger himself. Unfortunately he'd already set off in pursuit of the noise, self-preservation at the back of his mind.

Drawing closer, the trees thinned to reveal a lonely little cottage. In front of the humble building a woman stood before two young children, arms held wide to shield them with her own body. The three cried and begged while a man held onto an older child, seemingly playing a tug-o-war with the boy being pulled on the other side by a laughing duo.

"Please, no." The man begged.

"You know the law." The female aggravator said with a scornful laugh. "Sacrifices must be provided."

"No, please, not my son. Take me instead."

The heartless woman shook her head smiling, finding his distress highly amusing. They all cried and begged, and some even swore and fought back, but the result was always the same, when a witch demanded a sacrifice that demand had to be met.

Hunter had seen enough.

"Release him." He shouted with all the authority he once possessed.

The two aggressors turned, unimpressed by this scruffy stranger that dared to intercede.

"Move on." The male warned. "This does not concern you."

"Release him." Hunter repeated. "Or I will be forced to take action."

The crying father looked between the two witches and this unknown hero, his troubled mind slow to catch up.

"No signor, you mustn't, they... they will come, they will protect us." His strange mumblings faded into a whisper and he closed his eyes briefly in a silent prayer.

The man and his comments were ignored as the witches turned to the one individual willing to stand up against them, willing to fight even.

Hunter felt that familiar spark in his mind that sensed magic. Indeed the build up from the two witches was

194

almost tangible. He frowned, his hand clasping the metal amulet at his throat, his whole body reaching instinctively for protection. It had been years since Hunter had first used the natural shield that he was equipped with, and now it slipped over him with an invisible, but comfortable weight.

The first wave of spells hit, designed to blind and unbalance, a typical opening move. The magic distilled uselessly in the air, leaving Hunter unaffected and the witches disturbed and confused.

Hunter sighed, soon he'd draw his gun, he'd fight to destroy these ungodly creatures. But first he needed to protect the others in case things got ugly. With a simple thought he extended the shield to protect the cowering family.

Hunter snapped to attention, his shield was blocked, he pushed again but it felt like it had come up against a solid wall. This was unsettling, in the last two years, in the endless fights and battles his shield had been battered and weakened, but never blocked.

The spells came in from all sides, Hunter felt the shield buckle under the sheer pressure, he was half-aware of the witch-hunters at the very edge, no longer safe as his strength failed. Soon they began to fall, no longer protected from the lethal magic…

Hunter shook his head, determined to stay in the present. Another spell dissolved against the shield. Hunter frowned, he hated blood and death and had seen enough of both to last ten lifetimes, but he duly drew his gun and steadily fired at both witches.

Hunter heard a feral snarl rip from one of the witches, but neither of them fell. Hunter froze - his aim was infallible, yet they weren't hit. Even more disturbing was the expression of confusion that was mirrored in the witches' faces. The bullets had been stopped and it was not their doing.

Beyond the sound of his own thudding pulse Hunter became aware of a low hum of noise coming from the forest. He turned, automatically strengthening the shield about him. Out of the trees stepped two men, one grey-haired and wrinkled, the other younger than Hunter. Their eyes were closed in concentration and both chanted in low tones, the sound akin to a hum.

The older man suddenly fell silent and opened his eyes, facing the two witches. With a move of his hand there was a deep rumble and a bright flash of light. Hunter heard a scream rip from the witches, and he stumbled back, unbalanced and blinded.

It was over in a flash, Hunter felt his heart falter, then double its beat. The witches were nowhere to be seen. The father and son scrambled back to their family's embrace.

The two mysterious men turned to face Hunter, the old man locked his pale blue gaze onto Hunter and raised his hand… then faltered. His wrinkled brow creased further in a frown. He spoke quickly, but Hunter failed to follow his words, they were an Italian dialect he'd never heard before.

"Wh-what? I'm sorry, I don't understand." He stuttered breathlessly, unable to find his usual manners in this confusion.

The younger man looked at him with surprise. "Inglese." He said with some amazement, throwing a meaningful look to the elder.

"English? He says 'you are not a witch'." The young man explained in broken English, the words flavoured with accent, while he gazed curiously at Hunter.

Hunter wavered beneath those bright blue eyes. "No… I mean, yes I'm English. But I'm not a witch."

The older man whispered something to the young one, who nodded seriously.

"But you are using magic." He insisted, his eyes drifting along Hunter's aura, as though physically seeing the shield.

"Oh." Hunter turned his attention to his shield, reluctantly letting it drop. He was far from trusting these strangers, but felt he needed to show faith if he were to get answers. "That's not magic, it's something… different. I'm sorry, but who are you?"

"I am Marcus." The young man replied readily, a hand placed on his chest. "And my friend is Maurizio, we are Donili. And you?"

"Donili?" Hunter jumped at the word. "Of the Donili monks? But I came this way looking for you."

Marcus frowned, and relayed this to the older Maurizio, then turned back to Hunter. "And your name?" He insisted.

"Hunter Astley, a 7th gen witch-hunter with the British Malleus Maleficarum Council." Hunter replied.

Marcus hesitated at this stream of information, then repeated it to Maurizio. Hunter waited impatiently as they exchanged comments in that incomprehensible Italian, his nerves still sparking at every slight sound or movement.

"You will come with us, signor? Our council will have many questions. You have many questions also?" Marcus' voice rose, but Hunter couldn't tell whether in query or anticipation.

"Yes. Yes, of course." Hunter replied immediately, feeling truly hopeful for the first time in three months.

Maurizio, pleased with the outcome of this laboured conversation, turned to the family. The old man quickly exchanged words with the mother and father, and less quickly stood smiling as he accepted their thanks and blessings.

Marcus smiled indulgently, then hurried the older man along. They set off into the forest, trudging over the undulating ground. Hunter, used to his above average stamina and physical ability, was surprised by Marcus, and especially the older Maurizio, who paced along swiftly and untiring. Hunter came up with mental excuses, that he was wearied from being on the run for so long, that he was further tired by the brief fight with the witches - but the truth was it was embarrassing that his breathing grew heavier and he felt sweat run down his face and neck.

Hunter stopped to take a much needed drink from his old water bottle. He coughed and spat, feeling guiltily unlike a gentleman.

"How much further is it?" He asked his travelling companions, not quite sure what 'it' was. He took the opportunity to take a few deep breaths and kept his voice strong at least.

"Not far. One kilometre, no more than two." Marcus replied, patiently waiting for his English guest. He hesitated, obviously taking in Hunter's sweaty appearance and strained eyes.

Marcus turned and quickly fell into conversation with Maurizio. Hunter didn't even try to follow the flow of words, but he gathered from the stress in Marcus' voice that the younger man was trying to persuade the older.

Eventually Maurizio shrugged noncommittally and Marcus turned back to Hunter with a smile.

"We go the fast way - this is how we travel. Hold my arm. Trust me." Marcus said, holding out his hand invitingly, but an almost mischievous look in his eye.

Warily Hunter raised his hand. As soon as he touched the young man's forearm the world went black and Hunter felt a familiar shift.

Two

In no time at all, the world returned and Hunter saw an array of stone and brick buildings and heard the small crowd of people that turned to gaze calmly at the sudden appearance of three men. Hunter, so suspicious and tense himself, noticed that people looked at him with only a vague curiosity before moving on, as though their appearance were a common thing.

Next to Hunter, Marcus turned with an expectant look.

"Do you want to sit? It is disorie- dees... disorientante for new people." He said, but his smile faltered as he saw Hunter show no sign of distress from this almost magical form of transport.

"No, I'm fine thank you. Where are we?" Hunter asked, brushing aside the unnecessary concern and gazing about the settlement. The buildings were strong and sturdy and defied the forest which turned the horizon green in every direction. The land sloped gently downhill in front of him and Hunter could see the shimmer of a river where the houses gave way, and further the land rose again to the next sunlit hill. "Are we still in Friuli?"

"Yes." Marcus answered, still eyeing Hunter warily. "This is the village of Donili. Come, you must meet our Abate. He is at the abbazia."

Marcus led back up the hill towards a long, low stone building that looked down on the village like a guardian. Marcus glanced again at Hunter. "You sure you ok? Most people panico after their first travel."

"It wasn't my first time." Hunter said carefully, thinking this was enough honesty. There was no need to.

He didn't know how much he could trust Marcus and decided that the less he revealed about himself the better.

Hunter ignored the quizzical look from his young companion, and kept his eyes trained on the path, the last thing he wanted was to trip, fall, and look a prat. At one point, Hunter finally noticed the absence of Maurizio. But they had just reached the doors and he had no time to give the old man any further thought. Marcus rapped on the wooden doors and they were pulled open from the inside by a monk who nodded them through.

They stepped into a large courtyard. Hunter was struck by the simple beauty of the place; the sun warmed the soft brown stone, and along each side of the courtyard shadowed walkways were marked out with pillars.

Hunter heard the pad of soft shoes across the stone quad. He turned to see another monk approach them, the man looked young and strong, and he greeted them both with quiet confidence.

"Welcome to the Abbazia di Donili, Signor Astley. My name is Biagio, if you come with me I shall show you to the padre."

Hunter was briefly taken aback by his fluent, yet accented English and could only nod in reply, before finally coughing out a thank you.

Biagio smiled indulgently, then bowed briefly to Marcus before turning and walking away.

Hunter hesitated, not sure if he were meant to follow. He glanced at Marcus, somehow trusting this Donili monk that he met first.

Marcus tried an encouraging smile. "Perhaps I see you later, signore." The young man bowed and backed away.

Hunter frowned, he'd been deprived of company for so long, it was tempting to latch onto the first friendly face he saw. He had to remind himself that, until he had answers and his life had gained some aspect of sense again, he should remain wary and taciturn, there would be time for friendships later, if there were time at all.

Hunter gripped the straps of his rucksack and stumbled along behind Biagio, looking like any other weary traveller behind the quiet, composed monk.

Biagio led indoors and down a narrow stone corridor. He opened the last door and invited Hunter in.

Hunter didn't know what to expect, he'd been so preoccupied with the finding of a link to the Benandanti that his mind hadn't considered any further.

The room was cosy, with an upholstered bench and several soft chairs. There was a grand fireplace, that was yet unlit, and the walls were lined with shelves of books. The atmosphere of the room reminded Hunter of his own private study or drawing room at home.

There were three men sitting in the room, all were grey-haired and bore signs of age. They were in quiet conversation, but broke off at Hunter's arrival, they looked in his direction and Hunter could see that age had not dulled those sharp, shining eyes that pierced him curiously.

Next to him, Biagio made an introduction in that bizarre dialect.

One of the monks rose from their seat and replied, his gaze flitting between Hunter and Biagio the translator.

"The Abbot welcomes you, Hunter Astley. Please be seated, you must have many questions. And after Maurizio's account of your meeting, we too have questions." Biagio relayed eloquently, a slight air of smugness over his own fluency.

But Hunter paid him little attention, he glanced again at the two seated monks and realised that one of them was Maurizio. So this was where the old man had disappeared to - coming to forewarn the boss while Hunter toiled with Marcus.

Ever since he had found out about his abilities, Hunter had steadily gained more questions and no answers. But right now he was speechless. In the awkwardness of his silence, he acted upon the invitation to sit down, sinking into one of the heavenly comfortable chairs.

The Abate sat also and spoke again.

"The Abbot would like to know what brings an English gentleman to the hidden valleys of Italy?" Biagio voiced eagerly.

"I... I came looking for the Benandanti." Hunter replied, getting straight to the point.

Hunter waited impatiently for this to be relayed.

"Benandanti? It has been a long time since any sought them. They were a branch of our family that were wiped out hundreds of years ago." The Abate said via Biagio.

Hunter sat up straighter, his pulse quickening as his hopes were realised. "The Benandanti were part of the Donili?"

"Yes, they were one of the largest families. They were discovered by Europeans and were killed by their narrow-mindedness. The Europeans saw the skills that were inborn and strictly trained to protect others, but instead of seeing it as natural they accused the Benandanti of devil worship and magic and punished them.

"Thankfully, the rest of the Donili remained undiscovered, and by the grace of God, have been able to keep protecting those that ask for our help."

Hunter sat there, absorbing this new version of history. He had hoped that perhaps some of the Benandanti had survived, he could never have dreamed that the Benandanti were only a small part of something bigger, older and perhaps stronger.

"Now, I have given you an answer, it is your turn."

The Abate frowned, equally displeased with the circuitous nature of speaking through a translator. He looked directly at Hunter, "Te parle italiano?"

"Si, fluente." Hunter replied, feeling those blue eyes pierce him.

The Abate quickly dismissed Biagio, who looked disappointed at no longer being needed.

"This is easier, no?" The Abate asked in steady Italian. "I dislike using a translator, but like many of my kin, I only speak the language of our fathers, and occasionally Italian."

"Si, padre." Hunter said, then couldn't help but lean forward. "But I have many things to ask."

The Abate raised a hand to stop him. "Of course you do, but it is my turn. How else am I to ascertain if we should answer your questions, unless you answer mine?"

Behind the gentle words, Hunter saw the unyielding stubbornness of the Abate on this point, and he sat back reluctantly.

"Good. Now first, our friend Maurizio tells me you used a defensive shield similar to the Donili's. How?"

"It's a long story." Hunter sighed. "I'm a witch-hunter with the English Malleus Maleficarum Council. We discovered a long time ago that the sons and daughters of witch-hunters were born with certain advantages against witches and magic. Just small things really, they are faster,

204

stronger, can perceive the use of magic and are immune to some spells - improving with each generation.

"I'm a seventh generation and a few years ago I was - ah - awoken to the fact that I could do more. I could travel anywhere in a blink, I can shield and block magic…"

Hunter broke off, there was more to it than a few tricks, his ability to shield himself and others had been a major factor in every battle. But Hunter was sure he was capable of more, there were times that things - inexplicable things - happened; what else could it be but an unconscious use of his power. He had a sudden image of a crumbling church, dead witches half-buried under the rubble. It was a dark and terrifying scene, but if he could harness that particular power, it would surely shift the balance of power away from the witchkind.

"Are there many like you?" The Abate asked, breaking into Hunter's thoughts.

"No." Hunter replied. "I'm the only one. That's why I came to find - well, you. There's so much I need to learn. And… and for your help."

The Abate brought his hands together and looked over his steepled fingers at Hunter, his bright blue eyes very serious.

"Certamente! We dedicate our lives to helping others. But the help they receive depends on the path they are willing to take." The Abate said cryptically. The old man then frowned, an edge of suspicion in his voice when he spoke again. "Surely the help and learning you seek are the same thing?"

Hunter dropped his gaze, suddenly inspecting the dirt on his hands, before remembering he was an English gent and witch-hunter and should not fear being assertive with anyone.

"Padre, I come to you as a representative of the Malleus Maleficarum Council. It cannot have escaped your notice that we are at war against the witches. I come to ask you to help us in any way you can. Become our ally and help us drive away the shadows."

The Abate sighed, as though Hunter had confirmed his low expectations.

"No."

The single word surprised Hunter. One word, with no deliberation or uncertainty.

"No?" Hunter repeated, as though the meaning of the word eluded him. "Can't you... will you at least consider it?"

"Signor Astley, we are not fighters, we are monks, we protect life. Oh, I am sure you have what you consider valid points to argue, but on this point, I will not be moved."

"You say you protect life - then protect those worldwide that are threatened by witches. Give your protection to those that will fight for a better world." Hunter leant forward; his speech impassioned.

But the Abate looked unimpressed and did not respond to this request. Instead he turned quite calmly to the other two old men in the room.

"Forgive my selfishness brothers, in hogging all the words. Perhaps you could voice your opinions to Signor Astley's request."

Hunter blinked, looking to the other aged monks that he had near forgotten.

The unknown monk spoke first. "Whether we are the shield or the sword, we shall not enter this bloody battle. Our prayers would be ignored, and our souls scarred if we stood by and watched you and your kin killing, knowing that we were the ones that enabled such murder and massacre."

Hunter could give no reply to such an answer; how could he, he'd just been labelled a murderer. He was surprised at how forgiving the Donili sounded about witches - surely, they couldn't turn a blind eye to such an evil force. Surely, they had been fighting witches even longer than the MMC.

"How can we help those that would turn on us?" Maurizio finally spoke, "It happened once before, when your people discovered a power they did not understand in the Benandanti. The Donili have long memories."

Hunter looked with surprise at the old monk, for some reason feeling betrayed by Maurizio's harsh and unfair prejudice. How could they hold a grudge over something that happened 500 years ago? Back when the MMC was a very different entity, its witch-hunters narrow-minded and devout on a religious scale. The modern MMC were much more controlled, fairly ruled by strict codes and laws. But... there came a seed of doubt. Hunter flashed back to when he had discovered his own unnatural powers, he'd been torn with fear that he would be condemned, even by those he called friends, so much so that he nearly kept this huge defensive bonus a secret as he and the other witch-hunters prepared for a suicidal battle against the Shadow Witch.

"That's ridiculous." Hunter retorted with a shake of his head, arguing against his own thoughts as much as the monks' words. He took a deep breath, frustrated, and ran a hand through his straggly hair. "It's not like it was, things have changed; the whole world has changed. I've travelled so far and seen so much, if you would just listen and-"

"We believe you, Signor Astley." The Abate interrupted curtly. "Indeed, you look so tired from your travels and troubles. Perhaps you would like to rest and gather your thoughts before we speak again."

At his words, Hunter felt a wave of tiredness wash over him, and was immediately suspicious of the three monks that sat with him. Hunter frowned and fought the fatigue.

"No, I don't need to rest, I need to keep moving." He stumbled over the words, concentrating on keeping his Italian fluent. "I must keep moving... they cannot be allowed to find me. I must move on to find those that will help."

"No, Signor Astley, I think you need to sleep." The Abate said with quiet confidence.

And Hunter felt the darkness of unconsciousness sweep him away.

Printed in Poland
by Amazon Fulfillment
Poland Sp. z o.o., Wrocław